Victoria Torres, Unfortunately Average
is published by Stone Arch Books,
A Capstone Imprint
1710 Roe Crest Drive
North Mankato, Minnesota 56003
www.mycapstone.com

Cataloging-in-Publication Data is available on the Library of Congress website.

ISBN 978-1-4965-3799-7 (library binding)
ISBN 978-1-4965-3807-9 (paperback)
ISBN 978-1-4965-3813-0 (eBook PDF)

Summary: Victoria Torres dreams of being cast as Juliet in her class's production of
Shakespeare's *Romeo and Juliet*. So imagine her disappointment when she's cast as
Friar Laurence, a bald old man!

Designer: Bobbie Nuytten
Image credits: Shutterstock: Derek Hatfield, (masks), Cover, eurobanks, 156,
Fourleaflover, (tickets), Cover, joingate, (book), Cover, Tashal, design element, Cover
Illustrations: Sandra D'Antonio
Design elements: Shutterstock

Printed in China.
009581F16

SO MUCH DRAMA

by Julie Bowe

STONE ARCH BOOKS
a capstone imprint

All About Me

Hi, I'm Victoria Torres—Vicka for short. Not that I am short. Or tall. I'm right in the middle, otherwise known as "average height for my age." I'm almost twelve years old and just started sixth grade at Middleton Middle School. My older sister, Sofia, is an eighth grader. My little brother, Lucas, is in kindergarten, so that puts me in the middle of my family too:

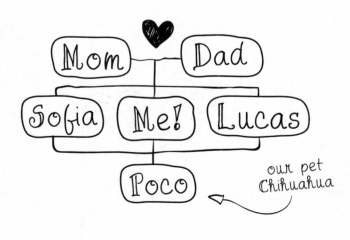

Mom · Dad

Sofia · Me! · Lucas

Poco

our pet Chihuahua

I'm average in other ways too. I live in a middle-sized house at the center of an average town. I get Bs for grades, sit in the middle of the flute section in band, and can hit a baseball only as far as the shortstop. And even though she would say I'm "above average," I'm not always the BEST best friend to my BFF, Bea.

Still, my parents did name me Victoria—as in victory? They had high hopes for me right from the start! This year, I am determined to be better than average in every way!

 Me!

Chapter 1

Java and Juliet

"Hey, Lady Vicka! Over here!"

Bea and Jenny wave to me from across the street as I hurry through the crosswalk to meet up with them in front of our local coffee shop, Java Jane's, after school. It's our new thing. We've been meeting here most Fridays lately, to treat ourselves after a busy week at school. It makes me feel very grown up to have a weekly coffee date with my best friends, even though the taste of coffee makes me gag! Fortunately, Java Jane's also serves yummy hot chocolate with whipped cream and chocolate sprinkles! Oh, and if you're wondering why they called me "Lady Vicka" it's because in Language Arts class we're studying the Elizabethan era, which happened in England about four hundred years ago. They liked to talk fancy back then.

*Un*fortunately, Annelise overheard Jenny, Bea, and me making our coffee shop plans today, so she invited herself along. Annelise is one of my sometime-friends. Sometimes she's nice, but usually she's bossy and insists on getting her own way. If she doesn't, she gets even. She invited her friends Katie, Grace, and Julia to come along too.

I'm running late because I had to drop off my little brother, Lucas, at my family's music store. Both of my parents are working there this afternoon and my sister, Sofia, had to stay at school for a student council meeting. It was my turn to babysit Lucas, so it was nice of Mom to say she could watch him for me so I didn't have to miss my meet up with the other girls.

"Good greetings, fair ladies!" I shout, rushing up to Bea and Jenny.

Bea does a curtsy and replies, "Likewise to you, my lady."

Jenny laughs. "My friends, I humbly beseech you to stop talking like that!"

We all giggle. "But Mr. Brighton will probably give us extra credit if we speak like Shakespeare outside of class," I say. Our Language Arts teacher, Mr. Brighton, is gaga over William Shakespeare. Shakespeare is probably the most famous playwrite who ever lived! We've been reading his play, *Romeo and Juliet*, in class. It's a tragic love story. It's also super famous. There have even been movies made about Romeo and Juliet—two star-crossed teens from fighting families who fell in love, got married secretly, and then took their own lives when things got really messed up. It's a very sad story, but life, unfortunately, doesn't always sparkle.

"Mr. B. isn't here," Jenny says. "Only that *tyrant*, Annelise, and her troupe of sidekicks—Katie, Grace, and Julia. They went inside to save a table."

Katie and Grace have been friends with Annelise for as long as I can remember. Julia started hanging out with them after her best friend, Megan, moved away a few months ago. Julia is just as pretty and popular as Annelise, but she's a lot nicer.

Bea nudges Jenny playfully. "Better tell Lady Vicka who else is in there," she says in a teasing voice.

I scrunch up my eyebrows and study my friends over the top of my glasses. "Who?"

"Don't have a royal heart attack," Jenny replies, "but your *Romeo* just arrived."

Bea giggles.

Instantly, my cheeks turn a brighter shade of pink. I know who they mean—my crush, Drew. He's the cutest, nicest boy in our class.

I shrug, casually, even though my heart is beating like my dad's snare drum. He plays percussion in a band called The Jalapeños. Uncle Julio is in the band too. He sings and plays the guitar.

"I could care less if Sir Drew is here," I quip,

stretching my neck to peek through the big front window of Java Jane's. I see Drew and his friends, Henry and Sam, carrying cups of cocoa and a plate of cookies to a table. Henry spots me and makes a zombie face. He's the biggest clown in our class. Drew glances over too. He catches my eye before I can duck out of sight. *¡Uf! Did he see me gawking at him?*

Having a secret crush adds a lot of drama to my unfortunately average life. I want Drew to know I like him, but I also *don't* want him to know. It's complicated, but if you've ever had a crush on someone, you probably know what I mean.

"Uh-huh, right," Jenny says in a sarcastic voice as I flatten myself against the coffee shop door, hoping Drew didn't see that it was *me*, Victoria Torres, spying on him. "You obviously don't care about him at all."

I smile bashfully at my BFFs. "Just don't say anything to Annelise and the other girls about my crush," I plead. "Annelise would have it all over school by Monday morning."

Jenny and Bea pull me away from the door so they can open it. "You have our word, Lady Vicka," Bea says as they lead me inside.

"Make haste, dudes, make haste!" Henry says to his buddies when he sees us enter the coffee shop. "This place is crawling with a plague of girls!" Henry picks up a butter knife from their table and swings it above his head like a sword.

Bea, Jenny, and I roll our eyes.

Sam glances up from his phone, then goes back to thumbing the screen. "It's just Vicka and them," he says. "They're not as bad as some."

Drew sets down his mug and waves us over. "Greetings, fair maidens," he says with a fancy accent that makes him even *cuter*. "What brings you three into our midst on this fine Friday eve?"

"Coffee and sweets, good sir," I reply with a curtsy. Talking to Drew like we're characters in a play, instead of classmates, keeps me from freezing up, or babbling like a water fountain that won't turn off.

But then Drew takes another sip from his mug, and suddenly he's back to being his normal sixth-grade self. "I never get coffee," he tells me, dropping the flowery accent. "I always order hot chocolate. Truth? Coffee makes me gag."

I gasp. "Me too! It tastes like furniture polish! Not that I've ever tasted furniture polish, but if I ever did, I'm almost positive it would taste exactly as bad as coffee. In fact, I would rather eat a *dog biscuit* than drink a cup of it. Once, my little brother and I *did* taste a dog biscuit and, actually, it wasn't that bad! Not that I'd want to eat dog biscuits every day or anything, but my point is, nothing tastes worse than coffee. We have a dog, by the way. His name is Poco."

I catch my breath, realizing everyone is staring at me like my head has just morphed into a television screen that can't be turned off. *¡Ay!*

"Are you sure you're not drinking coffee, Vicka?" Henry asks. He and the other boys snicker.

Bea links elbows with me. "Gotta go!" she says as she and Jenny pull me to the back of the coffee shop where the other girls are sitting in a booth. Thank goodness for best friends. You can always count on them to rescue you from total embarrassment!

We pile in next to Annelise, Katie, Grace, and Julia.

"What are you doing?!" Annelise barks as I squish in next to her. "You're supposed to order before you sit down."

"Um . . . I've lost my appetite," I reply, glancing back at Drew. He and the other boys have gone back to their cocoa and cookies. I breathe a sigh of relief. *Did I just tell my crush I've tasted dog biscuits?! Good one, Victoria.*

"Well, help yourselves to the brownie I ordered," Julia says, sliding her plate toward Bea, Jenny, and me. A brownie as big as a chalkboard eraser sits on it. "I'll get a stomachache if I eat the whole thing!"

"Thanks, Julia!" Jenny says, breaking off a corner of the brownie and taking a bite. Bea snags a bite too.

"Share and share alike, I say," Julia replies, smiling.

"Enough of the warm-fuzzy chitchat," Annelise says, pushing the brownie plate aside. "We have important business to discuss."

Bea, Jenny, and I glance at each other. "But this is *our* coffee date," I tell Annelise. "We're here for fun, not for a meeting."

Annelise flicks back her bouncy hair, knocking my glasses crooked because I'm sitting so close to her. She doesn't apologize. "We don't have time for fun today. Julia just told me that our Shakespeare Festival is at the end of the month!"

Every year, Mr. Brighton's sixth graders put on a Shakespeare-style party for their families when they finish studying one of his plays. When Sofia was in sixth grade, they served a banquet of food, played Elizabethan music, and put on the play *A Midsummer Night's Dream*. It was really magical and funny. Sofia was the student director that year. Mr. B. helped her choose the cast and organize the whole play.

"Earth to Annelise," Jenny says. "Mr. Brighton has been talking about the festival all week."

"He has?" Annelise says, giving Jenny a blank look. Annelise is usually too busy whispering with Katie and Grace or sneaking updates to her profile page to pay attention in class.

Julia nods. "I'm thinking about helping with the food," she says. "We could have giant brownies!"

"Yum!" Katie says. "Maybe I'll help with the food too! Or the decorations. I'm really good at art."

I turn to Annelise, straightening my glasses. "Why do you think we've been studying *Romeo and Juliet*?" I ask. "We're going to act it out."

"Duh, Vicka, I know *that*," Annelise says, tossing her hair again. "I just didn't know it was so soon. That's why we need to discuss who will play the important parts. Obviously, Drew should be Romeo. And *I* volunteer to be Juliet."

"That's not how it works, Annelise," Bea says, shaking her head. "There will be auditions for the speaking parts. You're going to have to try out if you want to be in the play."

I nod. "Mr. Brighton and the student director will decide who gets each part. I know because my sister was student director for her class."

Annelise stiffens. "But that's a dumb way to do it," she complains. "I'm perfect for the role of Juliet." She strikes an innocent pose and bats her eyes dreamily. "Romeo, Romeo . . . where are you for, O Romeo?"

Jenny snorts a laugh. "Wherefore *art thou*, Romeo," she says, correcting Annelise.

Annelise's sweet expression goes sour as we all snicker. "It's not my fault they talked weird back then," she snips. "The point is, Juliet has to be played by someone who is *sweet* and *pretty*." She bats her eyes again.

"Megan and I used to put on plays for our families all the time," Julia says, thinking back to when her

BFF still lived here. "It was fun, but I'd never dare to act onstage in front of a big audience!"

"It's not so bad," Jenny says. "I was in a play once, before I moved here. We put on *Cinderella*. I was one of the mice who pulled her pumpkin carriage!"

"There are no mice in *Romeo and Juliet*," Annelise says. "You'll have to help Julia with the food."

Jenny picks up a bit of brownie and nibbles it like a mouse. Everyone laughs.

"You should try out for the play, Jenny!" I say, ignoring Annelise's comment. "You too, Julia. Maybe you'll even get to be *Juliet*! You've already got the name for it."

Julia tucks her pretty red hair behind her ears and giggles. "What's in a name?" she says dramatically, quoting a line from the play. Then she giggles again. "I *do* like how the characters talk so fancy. Plus, the girls get to wear pretty dresses and veils!"

Annelise bristles.

"I love all of that stuff too," I reply.

Julia smiles at me. "You should try out, Vicka! You'd be great onstage!" She looks around our table. "All of you should try out. I'll even come to the auditions and cheer you on!"

"No, NO, **NO!**" Annelise looks like she's ready to explode. "If all of you try out, it will only bog things down!" Then she goes on to tell us, again, why she is the best choice for Juliet.

I tune out Annelise, munch a bite of brownie, and think about Julia's suggestion. *What if I did try out for the play? And what if I got the part of Juliet? And Drew got the part of Romeo?! I would get to share the stage with my crush! That would make me shine from the inside out!*

". . . so, as you can see," Annelise continues with her nose in the air, "it's a silly waste of time for you guys to try out against me."

"Don't worry," Grace says. "I'm not trying out for the play. Who wants to memorize all those lines? Not me."

"Me either," Katie puts in. "I've got more important things to do." She takes out her phone and starts texting.

Annelise gives Grace and Katie an approving nod.

But then Jenny says, "I'm gonna try out. But I only want a small part." She looks at me. "How about it, Vicka? You in?"

I bite my lip, thinking about wearing a fancy gown, standing on a sparkly balcony, saying sweet words to my cute crush.

"Okay," I say. "I'm in too!" Jenny gives me a high five. We look at Julia as Annelise stiffens into stone beside me. Julia shakes her head no, but Jenny and I do our most dramatic begging. Finally she says, "Well, maybe I'll think about it."

I give Julia a big smile, then look at Bea. "How about it, BFF? Will you audition with us?"

Bea thinks for a moment. "I'm not sure," she says. "I want to be part of the play, but I don't want to be under the stage lights."

Annelise sighs with relief. "Finally, someone is talking sensibly."

Suddenly a spitball lands on Julia's brownie! Then one hits my arm. Another one bonks Bea in the nose! We look over and see the boys cracking up as Drew blows through a straw and another wad of paper sails our way.

¡Uf! Boys can be cute and charming one minute and totally annoying the next!

Still, if I got to play Juliet, opposite Drew as Romeo, I could learn to live with his annoying side.

Chapter 2

Take That, You Venomous Toad!

"Thou art a most notable coward!" Henry swings a pencil at Drew, like a sword, in Language Arts class on Monday. "Accept my challenge, you venomous toad, and meet your fate!"

Drew pulls out a pencil too, and the two friends start dueling up and down the aisles of Mr. Brighton's room. Mr. Brighton has been teaching us insulting phrases from Shakespeare's plays. He says if you must insult someone, you should at least do it with style.

"Take that, you scullion!" Drew says, jabbing his pencil at Henry.

"You can't beat me!" Henry shouts back, dodging Drew's jabs. "Thou art a pigeon-livered coward!"

"And you, good sir, are a flesh-monger and a fool!" Drew replies.

Henry furrows his brow, grits his teeth, and lunges at Drew.

Drew pretends to go down, falling dramatically across his desk.

Everyone applauds, like we're at the theater.

Henry takes a bow.

"Call a truce, my lads," Mr. Brighton says from his desk. "Class is about to begin."

Drew looks up. "But I'm feeling better, Mr. B.! Let me have another go at him."

"Save it for the play," Mr. Brighton replies, getting up from his desk. "We'll need some good actors and fancy footwork for the fight scenes!"

As everyone takes their seats, Mr. Brighton walks to the front of the classroom. "Last week, we finished reading *Romeo and Juliet* and discussing the main events of that famous love story. Who would like to summarize the play for us in their own words?"

"I'll give it a shot, Mr. B," Henry says, setting down his pencil-sword.

"Go for it, Henry," Mr. Brighton replies.

Henry stands up, rakes his hair out of his eyes, and says, "Once upon a time, there were these two families, right? They basically hated each other's guts and wanted to do each other in. One family, the Capulets, had a kid named Juliet. The other family, the Montagues, had a son named Romeo. Kind of a flaky dude, in my opinion, but hey, that's life. Anyway, Juliet's family threw a big bash. Must have been Halloween because everyone wore masks. Some of Romeo's buddies tried talking him into going to the party, because he was lovesick over some girl named Rosaline. Only thing was, Rosaline didn't like Romeo back." Henry sighs and shakes his head. "Story of my life."

Everyone laughs.

"Continue, Henry," Mr. Brighton says.

"So, anyway," Henry says, "the Romester's friends figured he might meet someone new at the party and stop acting like such a mushy jerk. They finally got him to go. Since Juliet's old man was throwing the party, she was there. The Romester took one look at Jules and forgot all about ol' What's-Her-Name. Juliet was gaga for Romeo too, probably because he was wearing a mask . . . heh, heh. Anyway, they danced, they kissed, they fell in love. But they had to keep it all on the down low because Mom and Pop Capulet wanted Juliet to marry this other dude named Paris."

Mr. Brighton clears his throat. "Notice how the pace keeps picking up, adding to the drama," he says. "The characters are making quick decisions that will have serious consequences later." He looks around the room. "Who would like to continue the story? Felicia? How about you?"

Felicia sits up taller in her chair. Henry sits down as Felicia picks up where he left off. "Later that night,

Romeo and Juliet secretly met up on her balcony, and decided to get married the next day. An old monk named Friar Laurence volunteered to marry them because he thought it would make their families stop fighting and be friends. Romeo and Juliet figured everything would work out okay, too. But then Romeo sort of accidentally-on-purpose killed Juliet's cousin Tybalt. He didn't want to do it, but Tybalt had slayed Romeo's BFF, Mercurtio, so Juliet let it slide." Felicia looks across the aisle at me. "Your turn, Vicka. Go."

I bite my lip, trying to remember what happens next in the story. "The Prince of Verona, who was in charge of the whole city, kicked Romeo out of town," I begin. "Juliet's dad decided she had to marry Paris, ASAP. But he didn't know his daughter was already married to Romeo. That's when Friar Laurence real-ized he had a major problem on his hands. So he tried to fix things by giving Juliet a sleeping potion to drink. She drank it down that night, and the next morning everyone thought she was dead, but really she was just in a deep sleep. Only no one told Romeo. When he heard that Juliet had died, he bought some poison and went to her tomb. When he got there, Juliet really did look dead, so he drank the poison and died for real. But, just then, Juliet woke up and saw Romeo lying there. Friar Laurence tried to talk her into running away, but she didn't want to live without her one true love. So as soon as the friar left the tomb, Juliet grabbed Romeo's dagger and . . . well . . ." I bite my lip again.

"She took one for the team," Drew puts in.

I nod.

"Bummer," Grace says.

"Yeah, major bummer," Katie adds.

"The whole story wraps up with the Capulets and Montagues setting aside their differences and being friends again," Bea says.

Henry nods. "And everyone lived happily ever after. Except for the Romester and Juliet, of course. The end." Everyone bursts out clapping.

"Thank you for that highly creative summary, everyone!" Mr. Brighton says. "I can't wait to see how you all bring the story to life on stage!" Mr. Brighton picks up a clipboard. "We'll need a director, script writers, a stage crew, and, of course, the cast of characters. Some of your parents have already volunteered to help with other areas of the festival, so I will oversee the play. We don't have a lot of time to prepare, so we'll need everyone's cooperation. Our first order of business is to choose a student director." He looks around the room. "Any volunteers?"

Everyone starts buzzing about the festival. Some kids want to make decorations and plan the food. Others want to do music. I hear lots of talk about the play too.

Finally Bea raises her hand. "Mr. Brighton?" she says. "I've given it some thought, and I'd like to help direct the play."

Mr. Brighton smiles at Bea. "Excellent! You are our student director, Bea." He walks over to her desk and hands her the clipboard. "Next we need volunteers to serve as our stage crew. There will be sets to build, costumes to sort through from past plays, and a script to write. It's a long play, so I will help our scriptwriters whittle it down to the main events for our production."

Grace raises her hand.

"Yes, Grace?" Mr. Brighton calls on her.

"I dunno," Grace says, "but I've got really good penmanship. And, you know, my own laptop? I guess I could help write the script."

"Thank you, Grace!" Mr. Brighton replies. "Consider yourself hired!"

"I'll help Grace!" Katie chimes in. Grace smiles and gives Katie a high five. They do everything together.

"Bea, we have our scriptwriters," Mr. Brighton tells my BFF. "We'll also need someone to go through our costumes and props to outfit our cast."

Bea looks around the room. "Would anyone be willing to help with the costumes? Like Mr. B. said, all you have to do is get stuff organized."

"I'll do it," Felicia says. "I've got good fashion sense, obviously." She strikes a movie star pose.

We all laugh.

"You're on, Felicia," Bea says, making notes on the clipboard. "We're going to need some scenery backdrops and some kind of tall platform for the balcony scene. Who is good with paint, hammers, and nails?"

"Me," Eduardo says, raising his hand. "My dad works construction. I can get some tools and supplies. I'll round up some friends to help."

"Count me in, Ed," Sam says, volunteering.

"Perfect!" Bea says. "Thanks, Ed and Sam. All that remains, then, is choosing the cast." Annelise's hand shoots up. "I volunteer for the part of Juliet."

Bea shoots a worried look at Mr. Brighton.

"Thank you, Annelise," Mr. Brighton says. "But we will hold auditions for all the parts."

Bea breathes a sigh of relief. Annelise crosses her arms and slumps in her chair.

"In fact, I thought we could schedule the auditions for Thursday after school," Mr. Brighton continues. "That will give everyone a few days to practice."

Bea nods in agreement then flips through her copy of *Romeo and Juliet*. "We'll need lots of actors," she says. "Besides Romeo and Juliet, there will be parts for Juliet's nurse, Lord and Lady Capulet, Lord and Lady Montague, Friar Laurence, Tybalt . . ."

"Ooo!" Henry cuts in. "Let me be that mad dog, Tybalt! He gets all the good fight scenes." Henry starts waving around his pencil again. Then he stops and gives Drew a sly look. "Better let Drew be that heartthrob, Romeo, so all the girls come to the play."

Henry grins and pokes Drew with his pencil.

Drew gives Henry's arm a punch. "Knock it off, Hen," he says gruffly. His ears brighten when some of the girls pretend to faint over him. I'm not the only one who is crushing on Drew. If I got to play Juliet, and he was Romeo, I'd be the envy of every girl in my class! I bite my lip nervously and glance at Bea. She will make a great director. But would she choose me for the leading role?

"Like Mr. Brighton told Annelise, we'll assign roles based on the auditions," Bea tells Henry matter-of-factly. Then she tucks a pencil behind her ear. "Everyone who wants a speaking role should learn the balcony scene for the auditions—Act 2, Scene 2. The girls will read Juliet's lines, and the boys will read Romeo's. We'll need extras for the masquerade ball and the fight scenes, too."

Now Annelise jumps to her feet. "I would just like to say that I have acting experience."

Bea raises her eyebrows. "You do?"

"Yes," Annelise replies, lifting her chin importantly. "Remember? I was the Fairy Princess for our third-grade parents' program."

I remember that play. Our teacher wrote it. I was a caterpillar! My costume was a sleeping bag. All I had to do was inch across our classroom floor, pretending to munch on plastic flowers. I didn't mind though, because I was too shy to say any lines back then. But I'm not as shy as I used to be. And even though it scares me to think about having a big part, I really want to be in the play! And what if I did get a big part? Then I would shine for the whole year!

When the bell rings at the end of class, Mr. Brighton beams as we gather up our stuff. "We've got a great play in the works, class! Remember no role is too small. Every part is important. We're all in this together! With everyone pitching in, our play will be a smashing success!"

Chapter 3

Playing Favorites

After school, Jenny catches a ride home with her brother while Bea and I head to my house. We're planning to study for tomorrow's math quiz, but all we can think about is the play.

"I'm so excited to be the director," Bea says as we walk down my block. "But I'm nervous too. Lots of kids signed up to audition, including most of my friends. Annelise followed me around all afternoon, offering to carry my books, opening doors for me, grabbing pencils from my hand, and sharpening them before they were even dull! She's buttering me up like a slice of toast just so I'll pick her for the part of Juliet.

Other kids keep giving me sideways glances and acting super friendly too. I can't make everyone happy. Someone will be disappointed, no matter what. I don't want people to be mad at me. Then the play really will be a tragedy!"

"Don't worry, Bea," I say as we walk up my driveway. "You're always fair. Everyone knows you'll pick the best person for each part. And don't forget, Mr. Brighton will be there to help you."

Bea nods, but she still looks worried. "Did you hear Annelise talking by the lockers? She was bragging to her friends about being a shoo-in for the role of Juliet. I mean, she's pretty and everything, but Juliet is also supposed to be sweet and kind. Annelise is as sweet as a sour-apple jawbreaker. And *kind*? When Jenny finally convinced Julia to at least try out for a part, Annelise told her not to waste her time."

"What did Julia do?" I ask.

Bea shrugs. "She hurried away without saying a word."

"Annelise just wants to intimidate the competition so she can rule the play," I say as we go inside my house. Mom is at the music store this afternoon, so Sofia is in charge. I can hear Lucas's favorite show blaring from the living room TV as we get to the kitchen. I grab a couple of juice boxes and give one to Bea. "If Annelise were Juliet, she'd probably *trick* Romeo into drinking poison then skip the dagger scene so she could be the only star at the end!"

Bea giggles, taking a sip of her juice. Then she clutches her throat like she just drank poison and staggers around the kitchen, finally draping herself across the counter.

I play along, gasping as I pick up her juice box. "Poison, I see, has been Bea's timeless end," I say, ad-libbing Juliet's part from the end of the play.

Grabbing a spatula, I hold it up and cry out, "O happy dagger!"

Bea giggles, even though she's supposed to be a total goner.

As I aim the spatula at my chest, I hear someone say, "Have you two gone completely crackers?"

Bea and I look up to see Sofia watching from the kitchen doorway. As usual, she has a serious frown on her face. Sofia doesn't like to goof around.

I set aside my spatula and pull Bea up from the counter. "We were just practicing the death scene from *Romeo and Juliet*," I explain to my sister.

Bea nods, straightening her sweater. "We're trying to get into a dramatic mood because auditions for the sixth-grade play are later this week."

"Bea is the student director, just like you were in sixth grade," I tell Sofia. "Maybe you could give her some tips?"

Bea brightens. "Could you, Sofia? I'm desperate to do a good job."

Sofia walks over to the refrigerator and takes out an apple and then faces us again. "There's nothing to it, really," she says to Bea. "The most important thing to remember is *not* to play favorites with your friends. Give the best parts to the best actors, period." She gives me a sideways glance.

"Bea knows that!" I say, feeling defensive. "I wouldn't want a part I didn't deserve."

"Good," Sofia says, taking a bite from the apple. "Remember that when you get assigned the part of a chambermaid rather than the star of the show."

I duck my eyes and fidget in my sneakers. It feels like Sofia is dipping into my secret thoughts about getting the role of Juliet opposite my heartthrob, Drew. Unfortunately big sisters almost always know what you're thinking.

"What else?" Bea asks, soaking up Sofia's advice like a sponge.

"Don't let kids goof around too much at rehearsals," Sofia continues in her know-it-all voice. "You'll regret it on performance night. Oh, and don't freak out when things go wrong. And they will go wrong. When I was director, part of our set tipped over during the performance. You have to stay calm when stuff like that happens and then come up with a solution, on the spot. Mr. Brighton will be there, but *you* will be in charge."

"Got it," Bea says, keeping track on her fingers. "Don't pick people for the best parts just because they are my best friends. Don't let kids goof around at rehearsals. Be ready for anything to happen at the performance."

Sofia nods approvingly. "You've got good sense, Bea," she says. "You'll be a good director."

Bea smiles and takes another sip of poison.

Later, after Bea goes home, I'm thinking about everything Sofia told her earlier. I'm bursting to tell Bea how much I'd like to be Juliet, because we share all our secrets. But this situation is different. I want Bea to know I'm excited to audition for the play, but I don't want her to think I'm asking her to play favorites. I'd be no better than Annelise then, using our friendship to get what I want. So I've got to keep my mouth shut.

Like Sofia said, I have to be happy with whatever part I get, even if it's not the part I hoped for. All I can do is practice my lines and show up at the auditions determined to shine!

Chapter 4

Audition Day

When I get to school on Thursday morning, I toss my stuff into my locker, de-smudge my glasses, grab my copy of *Romeo and Juliet*, and clutch it to my chest. I've been practicing the balcony scene at home with Sofia all week. I know every single line by heart. But good old Sofia keeps reminding me that it won't be enough to just say the words perfectly. I have to *act* like Juliet too, or I won't convince Bea and Mr. Brighton that I was born to play her!

Then again, what if I *do* convince them that I can handle the lead? Can I really shine as Juliet? Or will it be obvious to everyone that they made a tragic mistake by giving me the lead? Will my performance be so bad it will seem like Bea was playing favorites?

I close my locker door and look down the hallway. Julia is talking with Annelise, Katie, and Grace. Bea has already dashed off to meet with Mr. Brighton so they can plan for the auditions. Julia has her hair fixed in a pretty braid that falls over her shoulder. She's wearing a flowery peasant dress and a sweet pair of velvety ballet flats. She looks like Juliet without even trying! But I just look like me: Victoria Torres, unfortunately average.

"Why didn't I think to dress up today?" I mumble to myself. "Julia looks totally ready to shine at the auditions, and she doesn't even want a big part! I look ready to eat tater tots in the lunchroom and study algebra in the library."

"What's the matter, Vicka?" someone says. I look away from Julia and see Jenny walking over from her locker. "You look worried about something. Plus . . . um . . . you're talking to yourself."

"I'm just nervous about the auditions," I reply. "I mean, it would be exciting if I got a big part in the play, but then again, I'm worried what will happen if I *do* get a big part. I'm excited and scared at the same time."

Jenny nods. "I feel the same way when I have a volleyball match or softball game. I want my coaches to put me in, but when they do, I'm afraid I'll mess up and let down the team."

"That's exactly how I feel," I say. "I don't want to let down the rest of the actors and, most of all, I don't want to let down Bea." I study Jenny for a moment. "Are you worried about the auditions?"

Jenny shrugs. "I already told Bea I don't want a big part. I just want to be in the cast, have fun at rehearsals, and put on a good show for the festival."

I sigh. What Jenny said makes a lot of sense. Why not try out for a small part? Then I'd be under less pressure, but I'd still get to have fun with my friends. Unfortunately, something inside me won't settle for that. Deep down, I want to shine as the star of the show!

I open my copy of the play and find the balcony scene. "O Romeo, Romeo," I say, reading my first line. "Wherefore art thou Romeo?"

Jenny grins, then nudges me. "He's right over there," she whispers.

I look across the hallway. Drew is standing with a group of his friends, laughing at something Henry just said.

"Stop teasing me, Jenny," I say. "That only makes me more nervous!"

Jenny keeps grinning. "Ah, don't be mad at me. I'm just trying to take your mind off your problems." She gives my arm an encouraging squeeze. "Just do your best, Vicka, nail the audition, and leave the rest up to Bea and Mr. B."

Jenny smiles confidently.

I give her a confident smile back. But just then Julia walks by, looking as breezy and beautiful as a fair maiden on her way to a royal party. Suddenly my confidence feels as mushy as a bowl of oatmeal.

Somehow I make it through the day without having a nervous breakdown. After school, we all gather in the auditorium for auditions. Lots of kids are here to try out for the play. Most of them look as nervous as I feel, which is kind of comforting. At least I'm not the only girl who feels like, at any moment, she might pee her pants.

Mr. Brighton is up on the stage, checking things over. Bea is standing down below, looking through some notes on her clipboard. She sees me walk in and gives me a friendly wave. Bea always wants me to do my best. She was right by my side when I tried out for cheerleading and when I ran for class president. But this time she'll be judging my performance.

"Good luck, Vicka!" Julia says, as she and Annelise walk up to me. "I know you'll do great!"

"Same to you!" I tell Julia while trying to ignore the stab of jealousy that pokes at my heart. In her peasant dress and braid, she looks like she just stepped out of a time machine that transported her here from an Elizabethan village.

Annelise makes a face at Julia and me, like she's been snacking on lemons. "Don't get your hopes up, ladies," she says to us. "There must be a dozen girls here, but only *four* female speaking parts in the play. If *I'm* Juliet, that leaves the rest of you to fight over *three* roles—the Nurse, Lady Montague, and Lady Capulet. Everyone else will have to settle for being townspeople or extra guests at the masquerade ball."

"I'd be happy with any part," Julia says, tartly. "Like Mr. B. said, no role is too small. Every part is important."

Annelise rolls her eyes. "He has to say stuff like that because he's a teacher. Everyone knows some parts are more important than others." Then she walks over to a chair and sits down with a flounce, like she's already wearing a fancy gown.

"I'm glad to see so many performers here!" Mr. Brighton says from the stage as everyone takes a seat. "Remember to speak loud and clear, keep your face toward the audience, and . . . have fun!"

Mr. Brighton looks at Bea. "Who will be our first pair on stage, Bea?"

Bea looks over the papers on her clipboard. "We'll start with Henry as Romeo," she says.

Henry's eyes go wide. "I gotta go first?"

Drew nudges Henry. "Go on, Hen," he teases. "All ya gotta do is *climb* a balcony and *kiss* a girl!"

Henry's jaw sags. The color drains from his face. "Muh-muh-maybe this was a bad idea . . ."

Everyone laughs as Drew tries to pull Henry to his feet. Meanwhile Henry goes completely limp like a sack of potatoes.

"Relax, Henry," Bea says in her director's voice. "There's no kissing in the balcony scene. There's no kissing at all. Mr. B. and I agreed we'll skip that part in our play."

Henry breathes a sigh of relief. "Why didn't you say so?" He trudges up onto the stage.

Bea looks at her clipboard again. "Vicka, let's try you as Juliet."

Now *my* eyes go wide behind my glasses! "B-but . . ."

Julia gives me a friendly nudge. "Go for it, Vicka! Show us how it's done!"

I gulp, but it's like swallowing sand. *I have to go first? And Henry is my Romeo?!* I like Henry, but he is the biggest clown in our class. There's no telling what he'll say or do on stage. I know my lines perfectly, thanks to Sofia drilling me, but Henry might decide to say something funny or do something goofy to get a laugh. That could throw me off. Why couldn't Bea have picked another boy for me to audition with?

"Um . . . any day now, Vicka," Annelise snarks from a few rows over.

Bea points to a chair that Mr. Brighton has set at the center of the stage then looks at me again. "Your balcony awaits, Juliet!"

Slowly, I get up and walk onto the stage. My knees feel like Jell-O as Mr. Brighton takes my hand and helps me up onto the chair—my balcony. The auditorium lights are on, so I can see everyone looking up at me as I stand there, like an awkward statue in the middle of the empty stage. Can they see my knees shaking? And the sweat prickling my forehead? My friends and I act out silly skits all the time at sleepovers. Just the other week, we pretended to be superhero girls fighting off the dastardly Lord Zit. I love to ham it up and be a real drama queen when I'm with my friends. But here, standing on my school's stage in front of my classmates and Mr. Brighton, it feels totally different. If I blow it, they might tease me all year!

As I'm thinking this through, Mr. B. sets another chair on the stage for Henry to crouch behind. "Our stage crew is building a nifty balcony and garden scenery for the play, but for now, we'll have to use our imaginations. Let me set the scene for you."

He walks over to the chair I'm standing on. "It's nighttime, just after the big party at the Capulets' mansion where, moments ago, Romeo and Juliet first met. Now the guests have gone home and Juliet's family has gone to bed, but she comes out onto her balcony, contemplating recent events."

Mr. Brighton pauses and looks at me, like he's waiting for me to say something, but I don't know what. "Um . . ." I finally say, giving the audience a weak wave. "Hi, I'm Juliet. Here I am, standing on my balcony, contemplating recent events."

Everyone bursts out laughing, but not in a mean way. It makes me relax a little.

Next, Mr. Brighton walks over to Henry, who is still crouching behind his chair. "Juliet's balcony overlooks a large garden with many trees and shrubs. Unbeknownst to her, Romeo is lurking in the garden, lovesick over his dream girl. When he sees Juliet on her moonlit balcony, he hides and listens to what she is saying."

"Eavesdropper," Sam shouts at Henry, which makes everyone laugh again.

"Yeah, if I were Juliet, and some guy was sneaking around my garden at night, I'd call the cops," Felicia puts in. "Either that, or sic my dog on him."

Henry gulps, then jumps up and looks around nervously, like a guard dog is about to bite his leg. The more everyone laughs, the less tense I feel. I guess it's true what they say: laughter really is the best medicine!

*Un*fortunately, my good feelings fizzle a moment later when Annelise's hand shoots into the air.

"Excuse me, Mr. Brighton," she says in a loud voice. "Shouldn't Vicka take off her glasses? I really don't think Shakespeare would want Juliet to wear them. She's supposed to look *pretty*."

Everyone gasps at Annelise's comment and then looks at me.

I know what Annelise is trying to do. She wants to upset me so I'll flub my lines. Then she'll have a better chance of shining the brightest when it's her turn to audition. I can't let her get to me. If I do, she wins.

"And what do you think of Annelise's opinion, Victoria?" Mr. Brighton asks me. "Do glasses detract from Juliet's beauty?"

I think for a moment. "I need my glasses to see," I reply. "In *my* opinion, it's more attractive to wear glasses than it is to bang into walls."

Mr. Brighton smiles. Everyone murmurs in agreement. Drew gives me a thumbs up! Annelise scowls.

I straighten my glasses and stand tall on my chair-balcony. Henry crouches low behind his chair-shrub.

"Okay, Romeo," Mr. Brighton says to Henry. "You're up first. Remember, you are head over heels in love with the fair Juliet. Try to get into a lovesick mood, then begin."

Henry nods and steps out from behind his chair, looking around the empty stage. "Woe is me," he says, trying to get into the mood. "I am so lovesick, and this garden is so dark." He pretends to back into thorny bushes, stumble over tree roots, and swat at bugs. "I sure hope I don't step in any dog poop out here."

Everyone howls with laughter. Even Mr. Brighton chuckles. "Nice ad-lib, Romeo," he says. "Now, how about saying your lines from the script? Look, there's Juliet, standing at her balcony! She doesn't see you, but you see her. What do you say?"

Henry looks up and reaches out to me. "But soft! What light through yonder window breaks? It is the East, and Juliet is the sun!"

All the guys snicker. But Bea gives them the stink eye and they stop.

"Okay, Juliet," Mr. Brighton says. "Your turn."

I clear my throat, face the audience, and say the line I've practiced a million times, as loudly and clearly as I can. "O Romeo, Romeo! Wherefore art thou Romeo? Deny thy father and refuse thy name; Or, if thou wilt not, be but sworn my love, and I'll no longer be a Capulet!"

A few kids snicker again, but everyone else is quiet, listening to me. I catch Drew's eye. He grins and my cheeks burn like I really *am* the sun, but I keep going. "What's in a name? That which we call a rose by any other word would smell as sweet!" Then I gasp, pretending I realize Romeo is watching me from the garden. I look at Henry and say, "What satisfaction canst thou have tonight?"

Henry reaches up to me again and bellows, "The exchange of thy love's faithful *cow* for mine!"

"*Vow*, not cow," Annelise corrects Henry, as everyone cracks up again.

"Oh yeah," Henry says, turning back to me. "The exchange of your *vow* for mine."

"If thy purpose marriage, send me word tomorrow," I reply, forcing the cow mistake out of my mind.

"All my fortunes at thy foot I'll lay and follow thee my lord throughout the world!"

Henry clutches his chest, then blows me a kiss!

It's not in the script, but I pretend to catch the kiss in my hand, then say the last line of our audition. "A thousand times good night!"

Everyone claps wildly as I hop down from my chair and take a bow with Henry. Even Mr. Brighton is applauding! So is Bea! They liked our audition!

"Well done, Vicka and Henry!" Mr. Brighton says. "You may return to your seats. Bea, call up our next pair."

My head is spinning with dizzy excitement as I sit down next to Julia and Jenny.

"You were fantablulous!" Jenny tells me as Bea calls Annelise and Sam to the stage.

"I hope I do half as well as you, Vicka," Julia adds.

I thank them, then try to focus on the stage. But I'm so happy and relieved to be done, I barely hear a word of Annelise and Sam's audition. Before I know it, everyone is applauding for them as they take their bows.

I've calmed down by the time Bea calls up the next pair. "Drew and Julia?" she says. "Take the stage, please."

Julia stiffens next to me. "You can do it, Julia," I whisper encouragingly. "It's fun, once you get started."

Julia nods, then takes a deep breath to calm her nerves, and stands up. I watch as she walks lightly to the stage in her flowery dress, then flits up onto her balcony, like a bird perching on a tree branch. If her knees are shaking, I can't tell.

"Begin whenever you're ready," Mr. Brighton tells Drew with a smile.

As Drew steps out from behind his chair and walks around the garden, all the girls in the audience start whispering to each other. He really does look like the perfect Romeo!

Julia gazes toward the stars, clutching her chest. "O Romeo, Romeo! Wherefore art thou Romeo?" Her

voice shimmers, high and sweet. Her eyes sparkle under the stage lights. "Deny thy father and refuse thy name! If you won't, swear that you love me and I will no longer be a Monta—I mean, a Capulet!"

"She said that line wrong!" Annelise blasts from the audience. "Doesn't she even know her own name?"

Julia winces.

Bea turns sharply and hushes Annelise.

Annelise sits back hard in her chair, fuming.

Drew and Julia keep going. When they finish the scene, we all clap for them.

"Well, done!" Mr. Brighton says as they come down from the stage. "Julia, I'm proud of you for not panicking when you made a mistake. Errors happen all the time in live theater. Not letting them get the best of you is the mark of a true actor."

"Thank you, Mr. Brighton!" Julia says breathlessly as she collapses into her chair again.

"*Pffft* . . ." Annelise snorts, crossing her arms over her chest. "*I* said *my* lines perfectly." Jenny gives Julia a quick hug. "You were great!" she says.

"Thanks, but I'm so glad it's over!" Julia says.

"But you didn't seem nervous at all," I tell her. "You were really good."

Julia thanks me, and we settle in as the next pair gets ready to audition. I can't help but think of how perfect Julia is for the part. She's pretty. She's sweet. And she didn't freak out when she said her line wrong. I look at Bea as she writes notes on her clipboard. Will she even remember my audition by the end of the day? Has she already decided who will play Juliet?

I catch her eye for a moment, but she doesn't give me any sign of what she's thinking. My best friend isn't sharing her secrets with me today.

Chapter 5

The Plot Thickens

The next morning, everyone races to Mr. Brighton's classroom before the bell rings. He told us yesterday that he would post the cast for the play first thing this morning. I was desperate to call Bea last night, to ask her who she and Mr. B. picked for the part of Juliet. But that would have been totally unfair to everyone else who had to wait until today.

Bea isn't at our locker when I get there, but her coat is, so I know she's here somewhere. I wait a few minutes and then figure she must have already gone to Mr. Brighton's classroom. Maybe she's going to read the list of names aloud? If that's the case, I better hurry. I ditch my stuff in our locker and hurry down the hallway.

A crowd of kids is gathered around Mr. Brighton's door when I get there. A sheet of white paper is taped to it. Something is typed on it, but I can't see what it says from the back of the crowd.

"Is that the cast list?" I ask Sam, who is standing in front of me.

Sam glances back. "Yep," he says.

I stretch my neck, trying to see past everyone. "Can you see what it says?" I ask again.

Sam shakes his head. "Nope."

Just then, Henry breaks from the front of the crowd. He's grinning from ear to ear.

"Are you Romeo?" Sam calls out to Henry.

Henry shakes his head. "No way. I'm Tybalt! Stand back people, I gotta practice my fencing moves!"

Henry starts swinging an invisible sword.

"It won't do any good to practice," Sam tells him. "You're gonna be toast in the end, anyway."

"Insignificant detail," Henry says, swishing his sword at Sam. Then he takes off down the hallway, telling everyone he meets that he got the best part in the play.

Henry's wish came true, I say to myself. *Maybe mine will too?*

The crowd creeps forward as more kids leave, talking about being party guests and townspeople. I overhear Min say she got the part of Lady Montague, but so far no one has mentioned Romeo or Juliet. There's still a chance my name is up there at the top of the list! I have to see for myself. I wiggle my way forward.

"Big surprise," Felicia says, as I squeeze in next to her. "Drew is Romeo."

"He is?" I say. "But . . . who is Juliet?"

"See for yourself," Felicia replies, pointing at the paper.

I crane my neck and read the first two names on the list.

```
Romeo:   Drew
Juliet:  Julia
```

My shoulders slump. Julia got the lead! Drew will be Romeo, but he won't be *my* Romeo.

"Oops, sorry about that, Vicka," Felicia says, seeing my face fall as I read Julia's name. "I didn't know you wanted that part too. Your audition was really good! You would have been a good Juliet too."

"Thanks," I say halfheartedly. "Not good enough, though."

Felicia pats my shoulder then starts to step away. But before she can turn to leave, Jenny pushes through, looks at the list, and then gawks at me. "That is so wrong!" she says. "You totally deserved the part, Vicka!"

I shrug, trying to hide my disappointment. "Julia deserves it too. Her audition was the best. Everyone knows it. And Drew will be the perfect Romeo."

"Don't look now, but here comes Julia," Felicia says, looking down the hallway. "I mean *Juliet!*"

We all turn and look as Julia walks up to our thinning crowd. "Is that the cast list?" she asks. "Henry told me it was up, but he wouldn't say if I got a part."

"You did," Sam says. "Congratulations! You're Juliet!"

Julia's mouth drops open. Her cheeks blush pink. "I am?! But I only wanted a small part!"

Sam shrugs. "Go big or go home, I say. You're leading the whole show. You and Drew."

Everyone gives Julia a round of applause as she stands there in stunned silence. I clap along too even though my hands feel as heavy as bricks. What Jenny said about me deserving the part may be true, but right now I feel as low as that caterpillar I played in third grade.

As everyone congratulates Julia, I realize I still don't know if I got a part in the play.

Turning back to the list, my heart sinks lower and lower as I read the names of the female characters.

Lady Montague: Min

Lady Capulet: Tara

The Nurse: Annelise

I scan the list of townspeople and party guests, but my name isn't there either!

"I didn't get the part of Juliet," I mumble to myself. "I didn't get any part at all!"

"Here comes Romeo!" Felicia shouts.

I turn to see Drew stop in his tracks as everyone singsongs, "Hi, Romeo!" in dreamy voices.

Drew raises his eyebrows. "Seriously?" he says. "I got the lead?"

Felicia moves aside so Drew can see the list.

"Congratulations, Drew," I say as he steps in next to me and reads through the names. "You'll make a great Romeo."

"Thanks, Vicka!" he replies. "Congratulations to you too."

I make a puzzled face. "What do you mean? My name isn't on the list. I didn't get a part."

"Sure you did," Drew says, tapping the paper. "You're one of the lead characters, just like me."

I look through the names printed at the top of the page, realizing I only read as far as Juliet. My jaw drops when I see my name, right below Julia's.

Friar Laurence: Victoria

"But that can't be right!" I cry. "Friar Laurence is a *boy's* part!"

"I'm playing a boy, too," Jenny says, pointing at her name on the list. "I'm Romeo's cousin Benvolio."

Drew smiles at Jenny. "Hey, Cuz!" he says. They laugh and do a fist bump.

I remember Mr. Brighton saying something about there being more girls auditioning than boys, but he didn't say anything about girls playing boys' parts. Even if Jenny doesn't mind playing Benvolio, I *do* mind playing Friar Laurence! Benvolio is young and funny, just like Romeo. But Friar Laurence is an old man!

As the bell rings, Jenny and Drew take off down the hall, still joking about being cousins. They're both happy with their parts, but I feel like I just got socked in the stomach. Bea would never make me play the part of Friar Laurence. This all has to be a terrible mistake!

Chapter 6

The Guy in the Middle

As locker doors slam and kids disappear into classrooms for first hour, I knock on Mr. Brighton's door. I have to talk with him, even if it means getting a tardy for my first class.

A moment later, the door opens and Mr. Brighton smiles at me. "Good morning, Victoria!" he says cheerfully. "I don't have class with you this hour, do I? Come to think of it, I don't have a class at all!"

I shake my head. "No, Mr. Brighton, but I need to talk with you right away. It's about the play."

"Certainly," he says as we step inside his classroom. "Is there a problem, Victoria? You seem upset."

"It's just . . . I'm happy I got a part in the play and everything . . . and it's okay that I didn't get the part I wanted, but . . . the thing is . . . there must be some mistake! My name is next to Friar Laurence."

"No mistake," Mr. Brighton replies. "You will be our Friar Laurence!"

"But . . . Mr. B., I'm a *girl*!"

Mr. Brighton smiles kindly. "Several girls will take on male roles in this production. It's not so unusual, really. Why, in Shakespeare's day the situation was reversed, with men and boys playing the female roles, since women were not allowed to perform onstage."

"I know all that, but the other parts are for *young* men . . . Jenny gets to be Romeo's cousin. Why do I have to play an *old* man who causes the whole mess?!"

"That's not the case, Victoria," Mr. Brighton says. "Friar Laurence helps everyone get along. He's the guy in the middle who ties the whole story together. Bea and I agreed that you are the perfect person for that role."

I shake my head, confused. *"Bea* thought I should be Friar Laurence too?!"

Mr. Brighton nods. "He's a peacemaker, just like you. You're always cheerful and willing to help. And your audition proved you were worthy of a big role. Trust me, Victoria, you will make our play shine!"

I want to believe Mr. Brighton, but my heart is pounding straight through my chest while he signs a pass so I won't get a tardy for my first-hour class. As I trudge down the hallway, all my plans to wear a beautiful costume and stand on a glittery balcony, saying sweet words to the cutest boy in my class, come crashing down around me. Plus, I'm going to have to marry my crush to Juliet! The day has barely started and already it's the worst day of my unfortunately average life.

"Where's that so-called best friend of yours?" Annelise asks crossly when I'm switching out books at my locker later. "I can't believe she's making me play the nurse! If Felicia tells me to wear one of those dorky nurse's hats, I'm going to die! It will completely flatten my hair!" Annelise tosses her hair like a horse's mane.

"You're not playing a medical nurse, Annelise," I tell her. "*Nurse* is another name for *nanny*. You know, like Mary Poppins? Only without the magic carpetbag."

"Oh," Annelise says, reclipping her barrettes, "I know that. But, still, it's dumb that I'm playing any part other than Juliet! I have way more experience than Julia. She didn't even want to be in the play!"

"You've been in *one* play," I remind her. "And Julia rocked her audition. Admit it, she's a natural."

Annelise crosses her arms and narrows her eyes. "A natural disaster," she mutters under her breath.

I frown, my glasses slipping down my nose. "What's that supposed to mean?" I ask, pushing my glasses up again.

"Nothing," she replies. "What part did you get?"

"Friar Laurence," I mumble.

Annelise's eyes go as wide as my Chihuahua Poco's when he sees a squirrel running across our yard. "Seriously?! I'd *quit* if they made me play him! He's *ancient*. And *boring*. That would be, like, the *ultimate* tragedy!"

"Thanks a lot," I sass. "I'm not quitting."

Annelise stares at me for a moment then bursts out laughing. "You're crazier than I thought, Victoria Torres!"

I turn and tromp down the hall. Annelise is the easiest person in the world to walk away from. *Un*fortunately, it's impossible for me to leave Julia in the dust. If she were rude and bossy, like Annelise, I could unfriend her in a minute and feel good about not wanting her to have the lead. But she isn't.

My grandmother—I call her Abuela—has a favorite saying: *"Los celos son malos consejeros,"* which is Spanish for *"Jealousy is a bad counselor."* As much as I want to wish for an epic outbreak of pimples on Julia's pretty face or a tragic case of laryngitis to silence her voice for days, I can't. She's my friend and, deep down below my disappointment, I want her to shine too.

All morning, I drag myself from class to class, wishing this day would come to an end so I could go home, eat supper, do my homework, go to bed, and wake up in the morning realizing the whole thing was just a bad dream! But it's only lunch time. I still have the whole afternoon to get through.

It isn't until I trudge into the Caf that I finally get within talking distance of Bea.

"Where have you been?" I ask, getting in line behind her. "Every time I saw you in the hallway this morning, you ducked away before I could talk to you."

Bea fidgets nervously as we wait for our food. "I know," she says. "I'm sorry, but I've been avoiding you. I've been avoiding everyone actually. I barely slept last night, worrying that half of the kids in our class would hate me for the parts they got. I didn't know it would be so stressful being the director!"

"No one hates you, Bea," I say.

Bea looks at me warily. "Not even you?"

I shake my head. "I'm upset, that's all. Mr. Brighton told me why you gave me the part of Friar Laurence. I'm just trying to get used to the idea."

Bea lets out a big breath like someone just lifted a piano off of her. "I'm so glad you don't hate me! We knew you were too good for one of the smaller roles. And, well, there aren't many female parts in the play. I'm sorry we didn't choose you for Juliet. Your audition was awesome! And I know Julia only wanted a small part, but she and Drew seemed like a good match on stage. I think they'll work really well together."

"You're right," I say. "They will be make a great pair, as long as Annelise's prediction doesn't come true."

"What do you mean?" Bea asks as we pick up our trays of food and walk to a table.

I shrug. "She's really mad about Julia beating her out of the lead. She said the play will be a disaster because of it."

Bea thinks this through, then brushes it off. "The play will be great. Annelise got a big part too. She should be happy."

"I know that, and you know that," I say. "But Annelise is never happy unless everything goes her way."

Chapter 7

A Rose by Any Other Name

When I finally get home at the end of the day, Lucas is caught up in some video game about mathematical pirates, Sofia is studying in her room, and Dad is still at the music store. Mom is working on her computer, but she stops typing when I walk up to her and burst into tears.

I kept my act together at school all day, congratulating other people on their parts in the play and pretending I was excited to be one of the main characters. But home is where you don't have to pretend. You can show your true feelings there, and everyone still has to love you.

After crying on Mom's shoulder for a few minutes, I calm down and tell her about my rotten day. "It's not fair!" I wail. "I knew my audition lines cold. I didn't get flustered when Henry was clowning around on stage. I faced the audience when I spoke, and I said my part loud and clear. So why can't I be the star for a change?"

"The star of the show isn't always the leading character," Mom says encouragingly. "You'll shine for all the reasons you just told me. You know the rules of being a good actor. You'll work hard to learn your part. And you won't get flustered onstage when unexpected things happen. Like it or not, Victoria, getting the role of Friar Laurence is an honor. The whole plot turns on the choices he makes. The play would be just another story about two lovesick teens if it weren't for him. Your character adds depth and purpose to the story."

"B-b-but . . . he's *old*," I stammer. "And *poor*! He lives in a *cell*, Mom. I wanted to wear a pretty dress and dance at the masquerade ball and say fancy words from a balcony."

"I'm sure the friar has some nice words to say too," Mom offers. "Let's hear your part."

I sigh, unzip my backpack, and take out my copy of *Romeo and Juliet* from class. "Grace and Katie are still writing the script we'll use for our play," I explain to Mom, flipping to Friar Laurence's first scene. "Here he is, entering his cell, which is probably damp and creepy, carrying a basket for collecting herbs because he makes them into potions and stuff."

Mom nods, listening.

"The gray-eyed morn smiles on the frowning night," I read. "Check'ring the eastern clouds with streaks of light."

"Well said, Victoria!" Mom says, smiling. "See? You don't need a fancy costume to say fancy words."

I have to admit, I like how Shakespeare describes things—calling the morning sky "gray-eyed" and the nighttime "frowning" is clever and paints a picture in my mind, even if I'm saying the words in a damp, creepy cell.

I skim ahead in the scene. Now Romeo joins me onstage and we have a conversation, just the two of us. This is when Romeo tries to convince me to marry him to Juliet. I can just imagine Drew standing there, looking like a handsome prince and me, looking like a frumpy monk. "I wonder what the friar wears, anyway?" I ask Mom. "Felicia is in charge of costumes."

"Probably something simple and plain," Mom says. "But that doesn't mean his character won't shine. Remember, beauty comes from within, Vicka, not from without."

I turn back a few pages to the balcony scene. "Here's my favorite line from the audition," I tell Mom. "Juliet says it from her balcony." I close my eyes and say the line by heart. "What's in a name? That which we call a rose by any other word would smell as sweet." I open my eyes again and look at Mom. "I'm not exactly sure what the words mean, but I like the way they sound."

"People did talk differently back then," Mom agrees. "But the feelings haven't changed. What do you think Juliet is getting at when she says those words?"

I look at my script and skim through the lines again. "I think she's feeling super frustrated. Because the only thing keeping her and Romeo apart are their names. If her last name was Smith or Olson, or even Torres, she could be friends with Romeo, no problem. But because she's a Capulet and he's a Montague, their families won't let them be friends. That's dumb."

"You're right," Mom says. "And unfortunately, that same attitude is still a problem today. Some people look down on others simply because of the family they were born into. Or because they don't like the way other people look or how they talk or how they choose to live their lives. For some people it's 'my way' or 'no way.'"

When Mom says this, it makes me think of Annelise. She always wants everyone to do things her way or not at all.

"Did you know Mr. Brighton asked Dad and me to help with the festival?" Mom asks.

"He did?"

Mom nods. "I'm going to pitch in with the decorations. Dad and Uncle Julio are teaching a group of students some songs from the Elizabethan era. They're going to dress up like troubadours and wander around the festival, playing music for the crowd. Won't it be fun to see Dad and Uncle Julio in feathered hats and ballet tights?"

The thought of my dad and uncle dressed that way makes me laugh! I just hope no one will laugh at whatever I have to wear. Mom said my costume will be simple and plain. Fortunately, plain can't be funny . . . right?

Chapter 8

From Bad to Worse

"Welcome to our first rehearsal for the play," Bea says after school on Monday. "Grace and Katie finished writing a fab script for us over the weekend. Mr. B. helped them cut-and-paste the main scenes so our performance will be short and sweet, and no one will have too many lines to memorize."

Julia breathes a sigh of relief. "Thank goodness!" she whispers to me. "As you could probably tell from my audition, I'm absolutely terrible at memorizing things." We're sitting next to each other on the stage floor, along with the other main characters. Annelise must have heard Julia because she looks over and shakes her head like she still can't believe Julia got the lead.

"I'll hand out the scripts in a few minutes," Bea continues. "But first Felicia is going to take you back to the costume room and show you what you'll be wearing for the play."

We follow Felicia to a big storage closet behind the stage. A bunch of costumes hang from a rod along the back wall—everything from old choir robes to Halloween getups. Big plastic totes sit on a shelf. One is marked *Hats*, another *Wigs*, and another *Props*. A fourth tote is labeled *Stage Makeup*.

"We'll keep the costumes simple," Felicia explains. "The boy characters will wear white shirts and dark sweatpants. Pull them up to your knees so they look like pants from Shakespeare's time. I found some cool hats from a pirate play that was done a few years ago. They'll look great during the fight scenes."

Felicia opens one of the totes and takes out some felt hats with wide brims. Each one has a

colorful feather tucked into
the hatband. Drew, Henry,
Jenny, and Sam try them
on. Sam is playing the
part of a Capulet named
Sampson. He's also going
to be the narrator. Jenny, of course, is Benvolio,
and Henry is Tybalt. They all have a big fight scene
together at the start of the play.

"Montagues rule, Capulets drool!" Jenny shouts,
sidling up to Drew.

"We could beat you Montagues with our hands
tied behind our backs!" Henry brags, standing shoulder to shoulder with Sam. They start a fencing match
out in the hallway.

The feathered hats look really cool. I peek inside
the *Hats* box as Felicia sorts through it, hoping
there's another hat for me to wear. But when she
turns back to us, she's holding three pretty headbands. Each one is wrapped with glittery ribbon.

More ribbons cascade down like long, colorful party streamers. "Tara, Min, and Julia," Felicia says, "you'll wear these headbands, along with your best party dresses."

The girls squeal with excitement as they try on the headbands. They do princess curtsies, then join hands and skip around in a circle like they're already dancing at the masquerade ball.

"Where's my headband?" Annelise demands. "The Nurse is a girl, too."

"The Nurse is a servant, so her costume is different," Felicia tells Annelise. Then she closes the *Hats* box and reaches up to the rack of costumes hanging along the back wall. "You'll wear this over a plain dress," she tells Annelise, pulling a long black smock off a hanger. "Put your hair up in a tight bun. We'll powder it gray."

Annelise's eyes go wide. "*Gray* hair? An ugly black *smock*?! I want to wear a party dress and ribbons like the other girls."

Felicia shakes her head and hands the smock to Annelise. "The Nurse is an old woman. Her hair is gray. We'll use stage makeup to draw lots of wrinkles on your face."

Annelise grits her teeth like she's wearing dentures. As Julia skips by, laughing and swirling her ribbons, Annelise glares at her. "This is *not* happening," she grumbles.

"It's no big deal," I say, trying to sound upbeat. "We can't all wear ribbons."

Annelise gives me a squint. "Julia should be wearing *rags* and sweeping the stage with a broom. *I'm* the one who wanted her part."

". . . and here's your costume, Vicka," Felicia interrupts, pulling a scruffy brown bathrobe from the rack. It looks like the one my dad wears on the weekends! "Oh, and this is for your head . . ."

She opens the *Wigs* box and pulls out something that reminds me of Abuela's swim cap. "What *is* it?" I ask, making a face at the weird, rubbery thing Felicia is holding out to me. Tufts of gray fur are glued around the edge of it, like a molting muskrat. And if I'm not mistaken, it sort of smells like a muskrat too.

"It's called a bald cap," Felicia says. "You'll have to wear your hair in a tight bun, too. Then put the bald cap on and tuck all your hair underneath it. I can help you get it on if you need me to."

My eyes bug as big as baseballs. "Are you saying I have to be *bald*?!"

Felicia nods. "Mr. B. told me that's how friars wore their hair back then."

I look at the bald cap. I look at the ugly brown bathrobe. "But . . . but . . ." I start to say.

"It's no big deal, Vicka," Annelise cuts in, mocking me. She snatches the bald cap from Felicia, pulling it down like a stocking cap over my head. "We can't all wear ribbons."

The boys and Jenny stop practicing their fight moves and look at us. "Nice hairdo, Friar Larry!" Henry jokes.

Julia and the girls stop skipping around and look at us too. "Oh, it's not so bad," Julia says to me encouragingly.

But I catch a glimpse of myself in a mirror that hangs on the costume room door. I look *worse* than bad! I look unfortunately *awful*!

Annelise shakes her head at my reflection. "See what I mean?" she says. "This play is going from bad to worse."

Felicia finishes handing out costumes and says, "You can leave your costumes in here if you don't want to wear them for rehearsals."

I gladly leave my bathrobe and bald cap behind. Annelise quickly ditches her smock too. But the other kids keep their feathered hats and ribbon headbands to wear for practice. Then we all go back to the stage where Bea and Mr. Brighton are waiting so we can rehearse the first act of our play.

Annelise, Julia, and I aren't in the first act, so we find seats in the auditorium. "This is so unfair," Annelise grumbles, slumping into the chair next to me. "I should be up there, wearing a fancy gown and ribbons in my hair."

"It's a fight scene, Annelise," I say. "No one is wearing ribbons."

"You know what I mean, Vicka," she says, scowling. "I was born to play Juliet!" She glances down the row of chairs to Julia, who is sitting by herself, practicing her lines. "*She's* the one who should play the old wrinkled servant!"

"Look, I don't want to dress like an old, bald man either," I tell her. "But complaining about it isn't going to change anything. The whole cast is counting on us to make the play a big hit."

Just then, Ed walks by carrying a folded-up table.

"What's the table for, Ed?" I ask him.

Ed stops. "We're going to use it for Juliet's balcony," he explains.

Julia glances over. "The balcony is a table?"

"Just wait till you see it. We'll paint a bunch of cardboard boxes to look like stones and stack them around it," Ed tells her. "When you stand on the table, it will seem like you're looking down from a balcony in your family's mansion!"

Ed smiles, but Julia's eyebrows crinkle with worry as she studies the table. "It doesn't look very strong," she tells Ed. "Are you sure it can hold me?"

"Positive," Ed says, setting down the table and unfolding its legs. "I tried it myself a few minutes ago. As long as these brackets underneath it are locked in place, the legs can't fold up." He slides four metal brackets toward the hinges that let the legs fold in and out. Then he sets the table upright and sits on it. "See? Rock solid."

Julia nods, but she still looks unsure.

"What would happen if the brackets came loose?" Annelise asks.

"Then the table could collapse," Ed replies.

Julia gasps. "That sounds dangerous! Couldn't I just stand on the stage?"

Annelise rolls her eyes. "If you're going to be a chicken about it, you shouldn't be onstage at all."

"Don't worry, Julia," Ed says reassuringly as he hops down from the table. "I'll make sure it's locked and ready before you stand on it."

Julia tries to smile.

Ed carries the table up to the stage.

Annelise watches him go, a hint of a grin on her face.

Chapter 9

Mask-Making

Fortunately, we didn't have to wear our costumes during rehearsal the past few nights, so I looked like my average self when Drew and I practiced the scene we have together, just the two of us, in my friar's cell. It's not as good as dancing with Romeo at a ball or blowing kisses to him from a balcony. But it's my time to shine with my crush, which is what I was wishing for all along, even if it's not happening the way I planned.

When a bunch of us get to Language Arts class on Thursday, we stop, frozen in the doorway. Mr. Brighton is standing by his desk, dressed from head to toe in a fancy costume, like I've seen people wear at the Renaissance Faire my family goes to each summer. He's got on a silky white shirt with big, puffy sleeves, a green vest with gold trim, green britches, long socks, and shiny black boots. On his head is a green velvet hat with a long white plume. Best of all, he's wearing a gold mask that's dotted with black jewels over his eyes. A bird's beak sticks out over his nose. The mask and costume make him look like a half-human, half-bird character from a fairy tale.

Henry fakes a gasp as we all pile inside. "Who are you and what have you done with our teacher?" he demands.

Mr. Brighton laughs heartily. "'Tis I, Sir Henry," he says in a Shakespearean accent. "Mr. B., at your service." Then he takes the mask from his eyes and does a deep bow.

Henry curtsies in return.

Mr. Brighton directs us to our desks, where plain, cardboard masks are waiting for us to decorate.

"Today, we'll begin making masks to wear during the masquerade scene in our play," Mr. Brighton explains. "All of you will be in the scene, whether or not you're part of the regular cast."

Mr. Brighton walks over to a display board that's sitting on an easel. A bunch of finished masks are tacked to it. "Here are some examples of masks my students have made in the past," he explains. Each mask is different. One is covered in blue and green feathers, like a peacock. Another is painted silver with elegant jewels dotting the edge and silver ribbons cascading down the handle that's attached to its side. A third mask is decorated like a butterfly with colorful wings.

A table is set up next to the display board. It's filled with art supplies—paints, brushes, glue, scissors, ribbon, feathers, sequins, jewels . . . everything we need to make our own fancy masks.

I, Victoria Torres, plan to make the fanciest mask of all! Mr. Brighton said everyone gets to be in the masquerade scene. This will be my chance to really shine during the play.

"The Elizabethan era was famous for its masquerade balls," Mr. Brighton says. "During a ball, the guests would dance, sing, and put on skits for one another. Young women were permitted to act in these skits at the ball, even though they were forbidden to perform anywhere else. The masks and costumes the guests wore were very elaborate and often depicted animals or mythical creatures. Shakespeare was clever to use a masquerade in *Romeo and Juliet,* because it allowed Romeo to get inside the Capulet house without being recognized as a hated Montague. It also allowed Juliet to let down her guard and join in the fun, dancing and flirting with the mysterious Romeo."

After Mr. Brighton says this, we all look at Julia and Drew. Julia blushes and turns away. Drew ducks his eyes and grins.

"For the next few days, we'll take time during class to work on the masks," Mr. Brighton explains. "Your mask should be a reflection of who you are on the inside, not necessarily how you appear on the outside. It's a disguise that allows you to be anyone you want to be!"

Everyone gets busy, sorting through the art supplies and taking them back to our desks. Mr. Brighton even lets us group our desks together so we can work with our friends.

"I'm going to make mine look like a butterfly," Annelise says, sketching wings on her cardboard mask. "I'm not afraid of heights, like some people." She shoots a sideways glance at Julia.

"My mask is going to be a bird, like Mr. B.'s," Drew says. "But I'll glue on some black feathers, so I look like a crow."

"You better make your mask extra fancy, Julia," Jenny says. "That way, *Crow*meo will be able to pick you out of the crowd!"

Everyone laughs at Jenny's joke.

"O *Crow*meo, *Crow*meo," Henry says in a girly voice, "Wherefore *caws* thou, *Crow*meo?"

Drew gives Henry a friendly shove.

"I'll use feathers on my mask too, so Drew and I match," Julia says. "But mine will be white like a swan."

"Ooh . . . *Crow*meo and *The Swan Princess*," Katie says dreamily. "You two really will be love*birds*."

Julia smiles shyly.

Annelise *tsks* her tongue and picks up one of Julia's white feathers. "Shouldn't you and Drew make *frog* masks?" she asks. "You both *croak* in the end."

Grace gasps. "Spoiler alert, Annelise!"

Annelise makes a face. "It's no secret they *die*, Grace," she snaps. "Don't you ever listen in class? Shakespeare gives it away at the very beginning of the play."

"Oh, that's right," Grace replies. "I wonder why he did that?"

"Maybe to make the audience really pay attention?" I offer. "Everything the actors say has more meaning because the audience knows it's all leading up to a big death scene at the end."

Julia nods. "But Romeo and Juliet don't know it. No one does, except the audience."

"It makes them feel like they're part of the action," Bea says with a spark in her eye, "even though they're not onstage."

"But it makes them feel kind of powerless too," I add. "Because they know what's coming, but they can't do anything to stop it."

"Excellent analysis!" Mr. Brighton says, overhearing our conversation. "Power is a crafty tool in this play. It tears apart families and makes for hasty decisions, but it also brings a whole audience of strangers together."

Annelise sighs, like she's bored. "Whatevs," she says. "My point is, the two *lovebirds* should remember nothing is going to end well for them."

As everyone gets back to work on their masks, I notice Annelise take the white feather she's been holding and tuck it inside her notebook.

"I'm proud of how hard everyone has been working on the play this week," Bea tells us at rehearsal after school. "I want to get through a bunch of scenes tonight. Vicka and Drew, you did great with your scene last time, but Annelise and Julia, you could use more work on the scene where you're getting ready for the secret wedding."

"It's not *my* fault we keep messing it up," Annelise says. "Julia can't remember her lines."

Julia winces. "I'm sorry, it's just that I have so many to memorize! I keep mixing them up in my mind."

"If the part is too much for you," Annelise says, "we can always switch roles."

"No one is switching," Bea cuts in. "We just need more practice." Bea looks over at me. "Vicka, since you're not in this scene, could you stand off stage and feed Julia her lines if she forgets them? I'd like to keep things moving along. We only have a few more rehearsals before the festival."

"Sure, I'd be happy to," I say, picking up my script and standing off to the side of the stage.

Julia smiles with relief. "Thanks, Vicka!"

Annelise smirks. "Don't worry about me," she snips. "I know *all* the lines by heart."

As Julia and Annelise go through their scene, I follow along, whispering lines when Julia gets stuck. She's doing fine, but each time she stumbles, Annelise sighs like it's a big deal. Poor Julia is a nervous wreck when their scene is over.

"Let's move on to the scene when Romeo finds Juliet in her tomb," Bea says.

"Good idea," Annelise says sarcastically. "Julia just has to lie there and play dead."

Ed rolls out a cart that's covered with a white sheet. Julia looks miserable as she climbs onto it and lies down. While Bea is talking with some of the other actors, I sneak over to Julia and smile encouragingly. "You're doing great!" I whisper to her. "Don't let Annelise get to you. She isn't happy unless she's bossing people around."

"I know, but it really upsets me," Julia replies. "I thought she and I were best friends! But friends are supposed to help each other, not put each other down. Do you know what I found on my locker door after school? A white feather was taped to it, with a note attached. The note said *Fly away, Swan*. I'm sure Annelise left it there. I recognized her handwriting."

Suddenly I remember the white feather Annelise hid in her Language Arts notebook.

"Annelise still has a lot to learn about being a friend," I say. "If we ignore her when she's acting like this, maybe she'll catch a clue and stop."

"Maybe," Julia says with a sigh. "I hope you're right."

"What's going on?" Annelise says, coming up behind us. "Giving Juliet a pep talk? It's a little late for that."

I turn on Annelise. "Stop being so mean. Julia has more lines than anyone."

Annelise crosses her arms. "If she can't handle the part, then she should step aside and let someone else take over."

"Places, everyone!" Bea shouts.

I dash offstage as Drew and Julia take their places in the tomb, and we run through the final scenes of our play.

After rehearsal, I help Ed wheel the cart offstage. Then I head to the costume room to see if Felicia needs help with anything. But before I get there, Julia rushes up to me.

"I hate to ask for your help again, Vicka, but if I don't learn my lines by next week, I'm going to get laughed right off the stage! Could you help me practice? *Pleeease?!*"

"Of course!" I reply. "Do you want to come over to my house on Saturday? Bea and I usually bake cookies on Saturdays. We can eat them while we practice."

Julia's face breaks into a big smile. "Thank you, Vicka! I'll be there!"

As Julia rushes off, Annelise shakes her head. "Why would you want to help the enemy?" she asks me.

I frown at Annelise. "Julia isn't my enemy. She's my *friend.*"

Annelise snorts. "She got the part we wanted without even trying. It would serve her right if the performance is a disaster."

Chapter 10

Practice Makes Perfect

While Bea slides the last pan of cookies into the oven on Saturday morning, I glance up at the clock. Julia should be here any minute to work on her lines. I've never had her over before, and I'm excited to see her today. Which is funny because just a couple of weeks ago, I was upset and jealous that she got the part I wanted. If she had asked me to help her learn Juliet's part then, I probably would have made up an excuse for why I couldn't practice with her. I might have even been secretly happy that she was having trouble remembering her lines. Sometimes when you don't get what you want, you want everyone else to fail too.

Jealousy is good at messing with you like that. I think it's still messing with Annelise. I'm sure that's why she left that feather and note on Julia's locker.

"*Arf! Arf Arf!*" Poco starts jumping around like one of Lucas's wind-up toys when the doorbell rings.

Bea and I race to answer it. Poco beats us there.

"What a cute puppy!" Julia exclaims when I open my front door for her. She crouches down to pet my springy dog. Poco hops right up onto her lap and starts licking her face like she's an old friend. Julia laughs, trying to hug his wiggly body.

I smile. "Poco likes you already, Julia," I say.

"I like Poco too!" Julia replies, setting him down again. Poco's tail wags like crazy as he leads the way to the kitchen. I wonder if there's anyone who doesn't like Julia. Other than Annelise, that is. And the only reason she doesn't like her these days is because Julia got the part she wanted.

The timer in the kitchen starts beeping. We take the last batch of cookies from the oven, grab a plateful, and head to my room. "Which scene do you want to practice first?" I ask Julia.

"All of them!" Julia replies. "But let's start with the balcony scene. It's my hardest one."

I move my desk chair to the center of the bedroom. "You can pretend the chair is your balcony," I tell Julia. "I'll read Romeo's part. Bea can be our audience."

"Okay by me!" Bea says, sitting on my bed with the plate of cookies on her lap.

Julia hands Bea her script. "If I forget what to say, just get me started . . . okay?"

"Got it!" Bea says, munching a cookie.

Julia steps up onto the chair, takes a deep breath, and begins. "O Romeo, Romeo. Wherefore art thou Romeo? Deny thy father and refuse thy name; Or, if thou wilt not, be but sworn my love, and I'll no longer be a Capulet!"

Even here, standing on a chair in the middle of my messy bedroom, with Bea munching cookies on my bed, and Poco gnawing a dog toy on my pillow, Julia says her part with lots of feeling, like a real actor on a real stage.

"That was fantabulous, Julia!" I tell her when we finish the scene.

"It really was," Bea chimes in. "I only had to prompt you a few times."

Julia smiles with relief. "I'm just afraid when I see all those people in the audience, my brain will freeze solid!"

"The auditorium will be dark," Bea tells her. "You won't be able to see anyone except us, your friends, up on stage with you."

"Really?" Julia says. "That makes me feel so much better! I didn't realize how scary it would be to perform onstage when I agreed to this whole thing."

We practice the scene over and over until Julia can say all of her lines with no prompts from Bea. Then Julia hops down from her balcony again. "If I can just ace the death scene too, then maybe I'll stop worrying so much."

"Great!" I say. "But let's take a break first, before all the cookies are gone." I slide a look at Bea. The plate on her lap is half empty.

"Oops!" Bea says, brushing crumbs from her shirt. "Help yourself!"

Julia and I sit on my bed too, eating cookies with Bea and talking about normal things like which TV shows we're into lately and which boys in our class are the most annoying these days and whether or not we're going to need braces when we get older. Then, when all the cookies are gone, Bea plays Romeo and I help Julia with her lines for the death scene. We practice it so many times I have her part memorized by the time Mom knocks on my door, asking if we'd like to come downstairs for lunch.

"Thanks, Mrs. Torres," Julia says, "but I have to babysit my little brother this afternoon. I better be going now."

"I didn't know you have a little brother too," I say.

Julia nods. "His name is Gus. He's in kindergarten."

"Cool!" I say. "My brother, Lucas, is in kindergarten this year too!"

"We'll have to have Julia *and* Gus over sometime," Mom says as we follow her downstairs.

Bea offers to help Mom set the table for lunch while Poco and I walk Julia outside.

Much to my surprise, she gives me a giant hug when we reach the end of my driveway. "I can't thank you enough, Vicka!" she says. "I know you were hoping to get the part of Juliet, so I feel guilty, asking you to help me. I tried asking Annelise to practice our scenes with me, but she acted like I had the plague or something. Every time I make a mistake during rehearsal, she rolls her eyes or laughs at me. I thought she was going to be my new BFF after Megan moved away, but now it seems like all she wants to be is my new enemy."

I give Julia's arm an encouraging squeeze. "You have lots of new friends, including Bea and me! Oh, and Poco too."

"Yip-yip!" Poco says.

We both giggle as Julia hugs Poco goodbye.

All week, everyone is busy getting ready for the festival on Saturday. Dad and Uncle Julio have been meeting with a group of my classmates at the music store after school, practicing Elizabethan music. Uncle Julio even learned how to play a couple of songs on a lute, which is like a guitar, only smaller. It was one of the most popular instruments in Shakespeare's day. Mom is stopping by the school, helping make decorations. Bea's parents are working with the food committee. Mr. Brighton told us that Elizabethan families like the Capulets and Montagues would have hosted huge banquets with lots of fancy food. For our festival, we're having a huge dessert table with lots of fancy cupcakes and yummy bars!

We're busy getting ready for the play too. Ed and his stage crew built an übercool set with a painted backdrop that looks like an old city with rows of shops and cobblestone streets. Juliet's balcony is finished now and under the stage lights the cardboard boxes stacked around the table look like a medieval tower! Julia's parents own the greenhouse in town, so they let us borrow a bunch of potted plants and shrubs for the Capulets' garden. Altogether, the set looks incredible!

Today, Friday, is our dress rehearsal! There's no time to meet up with my friends at Java Jane's coffee shop after school. We have to go through the whole play, in costume, without stopping even if people make mistakes. Fortunately, I have all my lines memorized perfectly. *Un*fortunately, I'm going to have to wear my brown bathrobe and bald cap for this rehearsal—*¡Uf!*

I've been preparing myself all day for the jokes and laughter that will come my way the moment I step onto the stage in my costume. But I can't let it bother me. Like Mr. Brighton said, the mark of a true actor is someone who can handle the unexpected moments that happen during a play.

At least I'll get to wear some sparkles for the masquerade scene. Felicia found a cape in the costume room that's midnight blue and covered with tiny silver stars. It's long enough to cover my frumpy bathrobe. It even has a hood so I can hide my bald head! When I put on the cape and my glittery mask, I look like a mysterious fairy princess, instead of an old friar. I can't wait to shine at the ball!

Julia is still super nervous she will forget her lines, so I've been practicing with her every day before school and during our lunch hours. We've practiced so much I know her part as well as mine! I'm still bummed I don't get to play the lead, but I'm happy that Julia and I have become friends. A play only lasts for a little while, but a friendship lasts forever!

Annelise is another story. Everyone is getting really tired of her constant complaining. When Julia and Drew are onstage together, she's always making snarky comments about how the scene could be better. The more we try to ignore her, the snarkier she gets.

"Here's your cup of poison, Drew," Felicia says when we all get to the costume room after school to get ready for our dress rehearsal. She hands Drew a little brown bottle. It looks like the kind my mom has in her spice cupboard at home.

Drew takes the bottle from Felicia. "Thanks," he says, opening the cap and taking a sniff. "What kind of poison is it?"

Felicia laughs. "You don't have to worry, it's just grape juice."

Drew takes a sip. "Yum!" he says. "My favorite kind of poison!"

"Give it to me after rehearsal so I can refill it," Felicia tells him. "I brought an extra juice box for tomorrow night."

"Gotcha," Drew says, closing the cap on the bottle. He starts to slip it into his pants pocket, then realizes his costume doesn't have any pockets. "What should I do with it until the death scene?" he asks.

"I'll look after it for you," Annelise says, stepping out of the shadows to join us. She must have been listening in. "My costume has pockets. I'll keep the bottle with me and give it to you right before you go onstage for the final scene."

Everyone shoots surprised glances at each other because this is the first helpful thing Annelise has offered to do for anyone in the play. I give Annelise a suspicious squint. What is she up to now? It can't be good.

"Thanks, Annelise!" Drew says, handing the little brown bottle to her.

Annelise drops it into the pocket on her smock. "No problem," she says. "I'm happy to help." Then she turns to Felicia. "Where are you keeping the extra grape juice? I'll fill the bottle for you."

Felicia smiles. "It's on a shelf, just inside the costume room door."

Annelise nods.

I relax a little. Maybe she is finally getting tired of bossing us around?

Our dress rehearsal goes great! Almost everyone remembers their lines, and I only hear a few snickers when I walk out onstage in my Friar Laurence costume. No one can believe how helpful Annelise is being. After the masquerade scene, she even offered to take Julia's mask back to the costume room for her so she could get ready for the balcony scene, which Julia totally rocked! After the scene, Annelise was right there again helping Julia jump down from the table in her long party dress.

And when it was time for the death scene, Annelise dashed out from behind the balcony and gave Drew his bottle of grape juice poison, just like she promised.

Drew chugged it down and, after the play, gave the empty bottle back to Annelise. Felicia even put her in charge of refilling it for the play tomorrow night. Annelise looked really pleased about that. I think she's finally putting her jealousy behind her.

Chapter 11

The Missing Mask

I look out from behind the stage curtain and gasp at all the people sitting in our school's auditorium. The night of our festival is finally here! The place is packed! I see my family sitting just a few rows back from the stage. Dad and Uncle Julio are still dressed in their troubadour costumes. They were so funny earlier, out in the lobby serenading people as everyone ate cupcakes and enjoyed the music and decorations.

My family is so different from the families of Romeo and Juliet. We fight sometimes, of course, but we always make up again. I'm thankful for the family

I have. I know they are proud of me even when I'm not the star of the show.

"Five minutes!" Mr. Brighton calls out as everyone rushes around, setting the stage for our opening act, gathering props, powdering their faces, and muttering their lines over and over again. "We'll take photos in the lobby right after the performance," he continues. "Keep your costumes on until then."

I pull on my bald cap, tuck in my loose strands of hair, tighten my bathrobe belt, and move off to the side, waiting for my turn to go onstage.

I see Bea, flipping pages on her clipboard, biting her lip nervously as she double-checks her list of things to do before the curtain goes up. Walking over to her, I give my BFF a friendly shoulder hug. She feels as stiff as a post.

"Relax, Bea," I say. "Everything will be fine."

Bea glances at me then back at her clipboard. "I hope that's true, but I can't shake this feeling that something bad is going to happen."

"Fret not, fair maiden," I say in my best Shakespearean accent. "Remember what Sofia told us? Unexpected stuff will happen. We'll just deal with it as it comes."

Bea takes in a shaky breath. "Thanks, Vicka. I wish I had your confidence."

Bea's comment makes me do a double take. Usually I'm the one in need of a confidence boost. It's nice to be dishing it out for a change!

Mr. Brighton walks up to us. "Is everyone ready, Bea?" he asks.

Bea nods. "I think so."

Mr. Brighton smiles. "Then on with the show!" He steps out from behind the stage curtain. The audience applauds. It sounds like thunder!

"Welcome to our sixth-grade production of Shakespeare's famous tragedy, *Romeo and Juliet*," Mr. Brighton says, greeting all our family and friends. "I'm very proud of our students. They've worked hard to put this performance together on their own.

There's nothing tragic about their teamwork! We hope you enjoy the show."

The audience applauds again, even louder than before. Mr. Brighton finds his way back through the curtain, gives Bea the thumbs up, then heads down the stage steps to take his seat in the audience.

Bea checks her clipboard, then turns to Sam, who is hovering nearby, along with all the other characters in the first act. "This is it, Sam," Bea says. "You set the tone for the whole play."

Sam gives Bea a nod, then turns toward the stage entrance as Ed raises the curtain. "Here goes nothing," he says. He walks to the center of the stage and bows to the audience.

"Two households, both alike in dignity, in fair Verona, where we lay our scene," Sam begins, motioning around the stage from the streets of Verona where he stands, to Juliet's balcony off to the left, and then to the graveyard that is lurking in the shadows on the right. "From ancient grudge break to new mutiny, where civil blood makes civil hands unclean. From forth the fatal loins of these two foes a pair of star-crossed lovers take their life."

Sam bows to the audience again, then draws his sword and joins Todd, one of his friends, for their funny banter about getting the Montague guys to start a fight with them.

"So far so good," I whisper to Jenny as she joins me offstage.

Jenny nods. "I just hope Julia can keep it together. She's such a good actor, but she's super nervous too. Felicia is helping her get ready in the costume room."

Some other actors run onto the stage now, challenging Sam and Todd to a fight.

"No, sir, I do not bite my thumb at you," Sam says to one of them. "But I bite my thumb, sir." He starts to suck his thumb like a baby. The audience laughs.

"That's my cue," Jenny whispers to me.

"Break a leg!" I tell her, which means *good luck* in theater talk.

"Thanks!" Jenny replies. She steps onto the stage. "Part, fools!" she shouts at Sam and the others. "Put up your swords. You know not what you do."

Now Henry runs in, swinging his sword at Jenny. "Turn thee, Benvolio; look upon thy death!"

Henry and Jenny begin a sword fight. It is one of the most exciting parts of our play, and Bea helped them choreograph it so it has some funny moments too. Jenny darts around like a hummingbird while Henry keeps losing sight of her. The audience laughs like crazy each time Jenny playfully pokes Henry in the back with her plastic sword.

They like our performance! Everything is going as planned so far. I glance around, expecting to see Annelise grumbling in the shadows, but instead I spot her smiling in her black smock and pinned-up hair. Felicia drew tons of wrinkles on her face, and powdered her hair until it was gray as a goose. Maybe Annelise really has changed her attitude for good.

At last, the Prince enters the stage and stops the fighting. Everyone exits the scene, except for Jenny, who waits for Drew to join her.

I look around again and see Drew, not far from Annelise. He's pacing back and forth, mumbling to himself. I've never seen Drew look scared about anything before, but now he looks totally terrified! Is this what they call stage fright? I don't know, but I hurry to his side.

"It's time for you to go on, Drew," I say in a low whisper. "Everything is going great! You'll do great too."

I smile at him, but this time I don't blush. Drew isn't just my crush. He's also my friend, and I want him to do well.

"Pretend it's just another rehearsal," I tell him. "And we're all here to have fun."

Drew nods, and takes a deep breath. "Thanks, Vicka," he says. His voice cracks with nervousness, but he dashes onto the stage.

Jenny greets him and Drew starts telling her he's lovesick over Rosaline. Once Drew gets started, his nerves loosen up and I can tell he's enjoying himself as he and Jenny make plans to go to the Capulets' party in disguise. As the curtain falls on Act 1, the audience applauds and Jenny and Drew dash back to me.

"Look at my hands!" Jenny says, holding them out in front of her. "I'm shaking like a leaf!"

"I was so scared, I thought I was gonna puke," Drew says. "But once we got going, it wasn't so bad."

"We better get our masks on," I say. "It's time for the masquerade ball!"

While the stage crew changes the set from the streets of Verona to the Capulets' ballroom, everyone finds their masks. I glance around, looking for Julia. I haven't seen her since we were putting on our makeup before the play. Maybe Felicia is still fixing her hair and fussing with her costume for the big moment when she and Romeo first meet.

Suddenly Felicia comes rushing up to me, with Julia close behind. "Where's Bea?" she asks, looking around frantically. "We've got a *big* problem!"

Julia's eyes are shiny with tears. "Someone massacred my mask!" she says, holding up the beautiful swan mask she made in class. It's totally crumpled and torn in two! Half of the feathers have been ripped away.

Just then, Bea hurries up to us. "Someone told me you were looking for me?" she says to Felicia and Julia.

They show her Julia's ruined mask. "It was on a shelf in the costume room after dress rehearsal last night," she says. "But when I went to get it just now, it was gone! Felicia and I looked for it everywhere. I finally checked the girls' restroom. There it was, in the trash! Someone wrecked it on purpose!"

A tear trails down Julia's cheek. I dab it away with the cuff for my bathrobe. "Don't fall to pieces, Julia," I say in a firm voice. "You'll ruin your stage makeup, and you have to look beautiful for the ball."

"I don't feel beautiful," Julia sniffles. "I worked hard to make that swan mask. It was my favorite part of the whole play! Someone must really hate me to be so mean!"

"Nonsense," Bea says, trying to sound calm and in control. "It was probably just someone's idea of a practical joke. Vicka is right. You have to pull yourself together and go on with the show."

"How can I?" Julia says. "The whole point of the masquerade ball is that everyone is wearing a mask!"

"Should we tell Mr. Brighton what happened?" Felicia asks.

"There's no time for that," Bea says. "He's sitting in the audience, watching the play. Are there any other masks in the costume room?"

Felicia shakes her head. "And we don't have time to make a new one."

"Here," I say, pulling my mask from the pocket of my bathrobe. "Take mine, Julia. It's not as pretty as your swan mask, but it will have to do."

"I can't take your mask, Vicka!" Julia exclaims. "You worked just as hard as me to make it. You deserve to wear it in the scene."

But I push the mask into her hands. "There's no time to argue about it. You have to shine the brightest at the ball. Don't worry about me. I'll find a way to blend in."

Julia looks to Bea for answers, but all Bea can do is nod in agreement. "Wear Vicka's mask. Hurry! The stage is almost set. The curtain will go up soon!"

Quickly Julia puts on my mask and dashes onto the stage. I zoom to the costume room, practically tackling Annelise on the way there.

"Watch out, Vicka!" she shouts. "You nearly crushed my mask!" Annelise puts on the beautiful butterfly mask she made. "We're supposed to be onstage."

"I know, but I need to find a *new* mask. Julia is wearing mine."

Annelise's eyes go wide behind her butterfly wings. "Julia is wearing *your* mask? Why would you let her do that?! It's not your fault her mask got wrecked."

I study Annelise for a moment, confused. "How do you know someone trashed her mask? It just happened a minute ago."

Annelise fiddles with the sleeve of her smock. "I-I overheard some people talking about it, that's all. You better hurry, Vicka. The curtain is about to go up." She rushes onto the stage.

I just stand there puzzling over Annelise's explanation and looking around for anything to use as a mask. Finally, I spot an extra script sitting on a chair. Quickly, I tear off one of the pages and fold it into a paper fan. It's not fancy, like the one Lady Montague carries, but it will have to do.

"Places, everyone!" I hear Bea shout as the stage crew positions the last cardboard pillar in place for the ballroom scene.

I grab my star-speckled cape, throw it over my shoulders, and wrap it around my brown bathrobe. Then I pull up the hood, dash onto the stage, and smile behind my paper fan as the curtain rises. Ready or not, here I come!

Chapter 12

So Much Drama

"Thank you so much for coming to the rescue with a mask for Julia," Bea says to me after we finish the masquerade scene. "Now if she can just get through the balcony scene. Do me a favor? Hide under the table she stands on and be ready to prompt her. She's still out of sorts over the mask prank."

"Your wish is my command," I say, giving my BFF a royal bow. I ditch my sparkly cape, grab a script, and dash to the back corner of the stage where the balcony stands. No one in the audience will be able to see me if I hide under the table because of the tower of boxes surrounding it.

But much to my surprise, when I get to the balcony, Annelise is crawling out from underneath the
table!

"What were you doing under there?" I ask as she
hurries to stand up.

"Nothing," she says, quickly. "I was just . . . um . . .
I had to . . . I mean, I dropped Drew's bottle of poison,
that's all. It rolled under the table, so I had to crawl
under and get it." She pulls the little brown bottle
from her smock to show me.

I squint, not sure if I believe her, but there's no
time for questions now. It won't be long before Ed
raises the curtain again. I start to crawl under the
table. Annelise grabs my arm. "What are you doing?!"
she asks.

"I have to hide under the table," I explain, trying
to wriggle out of her grip. "I'm going to prompt Julia
if she forgets her lines."

Annelise grips my arm tighter. "But . . . you can't!"
she insists.

"Why not?!" I ask, trying to tug my arm away from her. But the more I struggle, the harder she pulls back. "Because . . . because . . . it's not . . . I mean . . . I don't want you to—"

"Let go of me, Annelise!" I cut in.

"Not until you *promise* to stay away from that table!" She pulls even harder.

I twist and tug so hard we both half-fall against the table. It wobbles under our weight, then collapses to the floor!

Crash!

We both tumble to the floor too, bumping against the tower of boxes. It sways back and forth, then all the boxes fall down around us!

Smash!

Drew runs over from where he's waiting behind a bush in Juliet's garden. "Are you two okay?" he asks, throwing boxes aside and helping us get up. Other kids rush over too, including Bea.

"Oh my goshies!" Bea exclaims. "Is anyone hurt?"

"I-I-I'm okay," Annelise says in a shaky voice. She stands up and stares at the rubble of boxes around us.

"Me too," I add, straightening my bald cap. "The table collapsed, and then all the boxes fell."

"But that's impossible!" Ed says, pushing his way through the crowd. "I checked the table right before the play. The legs were locked in place."

"Well, somehow they got *un*locked," I say, shooting dagger eyes at Annelise.

For once, she doesn't have a quick reply. In fact, she looks too shaken up to talk.

"Yikes, Vicka!" Bea says in a concerned voice. "Were you under the table when it fell?"

I shake my head. "I was just about to crawl under it when Annelise stopped me."

Annelise gulps. Even with all the stage makeup on, her face looks grayer than her powdered hair.

Bea turns to Annelise and squeezes her arm. "Thank you, Annelise!" she says. "You just saved us from a worse tragedy!"

Everyone starts patting Annelise on the back, calling her a hero. But Annelise doesn't soak up the praise, as usual. She looks like she wants to be anywhere but here.

"I knew that table wasn't safe!" Julia says. "You don't expect me to stand on it now, do you?"

But Ed has already picked up the table and reset the legs. It's as sturdy as ever again.

Bea turns to the group. "Start stacking boxes, everyone," she tells us. "The curtain goes up in one minute!"

As we scramble to rebuild the balcony tower and Bea gives Julia a reassuring pep talk, Annelise just stands there, staring at the table, fingering the sleeve of her smock nervously.

Even though Julia is scared out of her socks to climb onto the table, we finally coax her to do it. Bea won't let me sit under it, though, so Julia is on her own. Unfortunately, she's so worried about the table falling again, she can barely remember her lines. But

Drew saves the scene with a lot of ad-libs and, somehow, they get through it.

When we help Julia down from the balcony a few minutes later, she's practically in tears. "I totally blanked out," she says. "I knew it would be a disaster if I played Juliet. Why did I ever let you guys talk me into this?!"

Annelise ducks her eyes and doesn't say a word.

My scene with Drew flies by. In fact, the next few acts speed by so fast that, before we know it, Ed is setting the stage for the final scene in Juliet's tomb.

I walk over to where Annelise is standing offstage. She still looks as out of place as a mouse in a room full of cats. "Are you sure you don't know anything about the balcony falling?" I ask her.

Annelise's jaw tightens. She shakes her head.

Just then, Drew hurries up to us. "Quick, Annelise, I need my poison!"

Annelise blinks, confused. "Your what? What are you talking about?"

"My bottle of poison," Drew says. "It's time for the big death scene. Did you fill it up again?"

Suddenly Annelise's face washes over with a fresh mask of worry. "Oh, no," she says, her hand flying to the pocket on her smock. "I forgot about the poison."

"No, you didn't," Drew says, reaching into her pocket and pulling out the little brown bottle. "It's right here!" He holds the bottle up to a stage light so he can see through the dark glass. "Good! You remembered to fill it with juice again."

Annelise snatches at the bottle. "Wait! I didn't . . . It's not . . ." she starts to say.

But Drew is already dashing on stage, the little bottle clutched in his fist, as the curtain rises on our death scene.

Annelise's hand drops to her side. Her shoulders sag. She starts rubbing her forehead like she has a big headache.

"What's wrong?" I ask. "Drew's got his bottle of juice. Everything is good."

But Annelise just shakes her head. "No, it's not," she says. "It's not good at all."

Bea hushes everyone backstage as Drew stands over Julia's limp body, says his lines, then holds up the little bottle for the audience to see. He uncaps it and starts gulping down the juice.

But suddenly he stops gulping and spits it out instead—all over Julia's pretty dress!

"Yuck!" Drew shouts, looking at the empty bottle in his hand. "That wasn't poison! It was *coffee!*"

The audience bursts out laughing as Drew spits and sputters again.

Julia sits up with a start.

"She lives!" someone shouts from the audience. Everyone howls with laughter.

Julia flies off the cart and stands there, gaping at her spoiled dress. Then she bursts into tears and runs offstage.

Bea motions for Ed to close the curtain then rushes over to Julia.

"First my mask gets wrecked," Julia wails. "Then the balcony collapses! Now my dress is ruined! This play is completely *cursed*! I didn't even want to do it in the first place!"

"You can't quit now, Julia!" Bea cries. "You still have to die!"

Julia crosses her arms and shakes her head. "I'm not going back out there!"

I turn and grab Annelise by the arm as she tries to slip away. "Why was there *coffee* in that bottle?!"

Annelise fidgets in my grip. "I . . . um . . . I . . ."

Bea takes Julia by the shoulders. "You *have* to finish the play," she pleads. "You're Juliet! We're all counting on you!"

But Julia pulls away, wiping tears from her eyes, smudging her makeup. "I *can't* do it! Someone else will have to be Juliet."

Annelise glances up, but then she looks away again. If she was hoping to upset Julia enough to make her quit, her plan worked. But now, after getting her wish, she looks like the most unhappy person in the world.

"Vicka," Bea says, turning to me. "You have to play Juliet!"

I raise my eyebrows so high my bald cap slips up a notch on my forehead. "Me?!" I exclaim.

Bea nods. "You know the part from practicing with Julia. And you've helped us out of every pinch tonight. You deserve to close the show. Will you do it, Vicka?"

Half the cast is huddled around us now. I look out at the stage where Drew is still sitting on Juliet's tomb, waiting for someone to tell him what to do. Mr. Brighton hurries up from his seat in the audience. "Everything under control, Bea?" he asks.

Bea looks at me again. "Is it, Vicka?"

Everyone is staring at me, waiting for my answer. I could say yes and save the show. Then I would shine like a real hero. But that would mean letting Julia give up. And friends don't settle for that.

I turn to Julia instead. "Please, Julia, you have to finish the play. If you don't, you'll always regret it. Nothing else bad will happen, I promise." I pause to look at Annelise. "Right?" I say to her.

Annelise ducks her eyes and nods.

I turn back to Julia. "You've worked so hard to learn this scene. I know you can do it! We're all here, cheering you on."

Everyone starts murmuring in agreement. "Come on, Julia," Sam says. "Let's finish this thing." He gives her an encouraging smile. We all do.

Julia looks around at all of us. She takes a deep, quivery breath. Then she looks at me. "Okay, Vicka," she says. "I'll do it for *you*."

As the stage lights wash over Drew and Julia a minute later, I hold my breath, waiting for Annelise to break her promise and shout something rude to upset Julia again. But she doesn't say a word. In fact, as I get ready to rush onto the stage for the final scene, she gives me a nod of encouragement.

"Go hence, to have more talk of these sad things," Sam says, closing the show. "For never was a story of more woe, than this of Juliet and her Romeo!"

The stage lights go out.

The audience applauds wildly. I think they're as relieved as we are to have made it through to the end!

"We did it!" Bea shouts, rushing over to give me a hug as the audience gets to their feet, clapping for all of us. "I couldn't have done it without you, Vicka." I give my BFF a hug back. As the stage lights come on again, everyone starts pulling us to the edge of the stage, holding hands in a line so we can take our bows.

Someone slips in line beside me. I look over and realize it's Drew! "Thanks for saving the show, Vicka," he says, taking my hand.

"It wasn't just me," I reply, shaking my bald head. "We all saved it, together."

Drew grins. Then he squeezes my hand.

I smile from the inside out as we take our bows, because a secret hand-squeeze from your crush can make you feel like the star of the show!

As the applause dies down and everyone starts breaking away to take pictures and find their families, Henry and Sam rush up to Drew. They tackle him with congratulatory backslaps and head noogies. "Dude, that coffee prank was genius!" Henry says to Drew. "I wish I'd thought of it."

As they gallop offstage together, I spy Annelise still lurking in the shadows, backstage. No one is congratulating her. No one is even talking to her.

"What do *you* want?" Annelise grumps as I walk up to her. "You should be out there, celebrating with your friends."

"What about you?" I ask.

Annelise scoffs. "I don't have any friends. Everyone hates me now, including you."

"I'm mad at you," I reply. "But I don't hate you."

Annelise gives me a cautious glance. "You don't?"

I shake my bald head. "No one does. Henry even thinks you're a genius for pranking Drew like that."

Annelise can't hide a grin. But it quickly fades away. "I didn't want to *hurt* anyone." Tears brim in her eyes now. "I was . . . upset. And jealous and . . . I didn't think things through." She wipes her eyes with the sleeve of her smock. "Julia and I were just getting to be friends. Now I'll never be able to face her."

"Yes you will," I say. "As soon as you apologize to her. And to Drew. And to everyone else. We're all in this together, remember?"

I straighten my bald cap, then tug on her arm. "Come on, Nurse. Let's finish this thing."

Annelise hesitates, but she lets me pull her along. We walk off the stage together, not exactly friends, but not enemies either. I guess you could say we're somewhere in the middle. Friendship doesn't come with a prologue, unfortunately. You just have to keep going along, never knowing for sure if it will shine in the end, but always believing it can.

About the Author

Julie Bowe lives in Mondovi, Wisconsin, where she writes popular books for children, including *My Last Best Friend*, which won the Paterson Prize for Books for Young People and was a Barnes & Noble 2010 Summer Reading Program book. In addition to writing for kids, she loves visiting with them at schools, libraries, conferences, and book festivals throughout the year.

Glossary

beseech (bi-SEECH)——to ask someone in a very serious way; to beg

consequence (KAHN-suh-kwens)——the result of an action

contemplate (KAHN-tuhm-plate)——to think about something

contrary (KAHN-trer-ee)——opposite

fluster (FLUHS-tur)——to confuse or disturb someone

insult (IN-sult)——to make a hurtful remark

intimidate (in-TIM-uh-date)——to threaten in order to force certain behavior

masquerade (mas-kuh-RADE)—— to dress up in order to disguise yourself at a party or other event

memorize (MEM-uh-rize)——to learn something by heart so you can remember it without looking it up

quip (KWIP)——a funny or clever remark

summarize (SUH-muh-rize)——to give a shortened account of something using only the main points

tragedy (TRAJ-uh-dee)——a play that is very sad and in which one or more characters die

troubadour (TROO-buh-dor)——a poet-musician of the Middle Ages in France and Italy

truce (TROOS)——a temporary agreement to stop fighting

tyrant (TYE-ruhnt)——someone who rules other people in a cruel or unjust way

Time to Talk

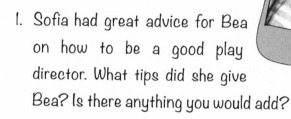

Questions for you and your friends

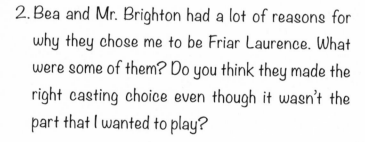

1. Sofia had great advice for Bea on how to be a good play director. What tips did she give Bea? Is there anything you would add?

2. Bea and Mr. Brighton had a lot of reasons for why they chose me to be Friar Laurence. What were some of them? Do you think they made the right casting choice even though it wasn't the part that I wanted to play?

3. I think it's super important to be supportive and encouraging. Do you think I did a good job of that while working on the play? Why or why not?

Just for You

Writing prompts for your journal

1. Think about the different roles that Bea and I had in the production of the play. Which role would you choose for yourself? Why?

2. Even though I wanted the lead part in the play, and I was upset that Julia got the part of Juliet, I still helped her with her lines. I had to put my jealousy aside and be a good, supportive friend. Have you ever been in a similar situation? Write about it.

3. We performed our play based on *Romeo and Juliet*. What book or play have you read that you would like to perform as a play, and why?

Word to the Wise

Standing up in front of a room full of people can be intimidating and scary. You might feel sweaty or even sick to your stomach.

But after you find the courage to get up there, it can make you feel strong and confident. So how do you manage to find that courage? Here are a few tricks you can try:

Tips for Overcoming Stage Fright

Practice your lines over and over. Being prepared will boost your confidence and cut down your worrying.

Try practicing in front of a mirror. That way, you'll know how awesome you look when you're onstage.

Focus on what you want to say and not on who is in the audience. If you focus on the words and how you are saying them, you won't have energy to freak out!

Be prepared and arrive early. If you are running late, you'll have a harder time calming down.

Think positive. Remember that the audience is rooting for you!

Take deep breaths! You've got this!

Cooking Corner

All that talk of brownies and cookies has my sweet tooth calling. Time to bake a batch of the best brownies. I like to cut them big enough to share with Bea or another friend!

THE BEST BROWNIES!

INGREDIENTS

cooking spray

½ cup flour

1 cup sugar

⅓ cup cocoa powder

½ cup butter, melted

2 eggs

EQUIPMENT

small bowl

9x9 inch baking pan

spoon

medium bowl

whisk

1. Preheat oven to 350°F. Grease 9 x 9 baking dish with cooking spray.

2. In medium bowl, combine flour, sugar, and cocoa powder.

3. In small bowl, whisk butter and eggs. Add butter-egg mixture to medium bowl and stir.

4. Pour batter into baking dish and bake for 25-30 minutes. Remove from oven and let cool.

MIX-IT-UP IDEAS

- Add colorful sprinkles to the top of the brownies while they cool.

- Drizzle caramel sauce on top of the brownies while they cool to add an extra, sweet flavor.

- Use cookie cutters to make the brownies into fun shapes.

- Serve the gooey brownies with some vanilla ice cream.

Victoria Torres

Unfortunately Average

Always looking for her way to shine!

Victoria Torres loves the family birthday party she normally has. But now that she's turning twelve, a family party seems average compared to the bash she could have with her friends at the mall's new spa store. Her mom refuses to let her have two parties and tells Victoria that's she's going to have to choose. Friends or family? Unfortunately, there's no easy answer!

When Victoria's band director asks for a volunteer to play the band's new piccolo, Victoria sees it as her shot to shine. Unfortunately, Bea wants to play piccolo too. The girls will have to audition for the spot, and the band members will select the winner. Can Victoria and Bea keep the competition friendly, or will their friendship hit a sour note?

When it comes to math, Victoria is completely average. But her sister, Sofia, is captain of the math team. When one of the team members drops out, Sofia must find a replacement—fast! Sofia volunteers Victoria and grills her in math, night and day. Can Victoria crunch enough numbers to lead the team to victory, or will her sister's bossy ways be too much to bear?

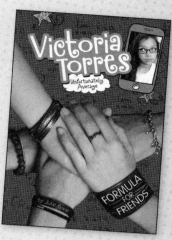

Victoria is positive being a cheerleader is the best way to secure her popularity. Her best friend, Bea, agrees to try out with her, but Victoria is going to need a lot more than Bea's support to make the squad. The competition is stiff and includes the awful Annelise. Will tryouts leave Vicka feeling far below average?

The sixth grade's choices for class president include Henry, who's only running on a dare, and Annelise, who's only interested in being bossy. Victoria Torres wants to actually improve the school so she throws her unfortunately average hat in the ring. But when the campaign turns dirty, Victoria wonders if the promise of shining as class president is even worth it?

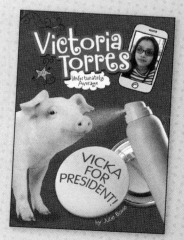

Find out more about Victoria's
unfortunately average life, plus
get cool downloads and more at
www.capstonekids.com

(Fortunately, it's all fun!)